Shadows from the Past

by

Rebecca Grace

This is a work of fiction. Names, characters, places, and incidents are either the product of the author's imagination or are used fictitiously, and any resemblance to actual persons living or dead, business establishments, events, or locales, is entirely coincidental.

Shadows from the Past

Cover Art by *Kim Mendoza*

The Wild Rose Press
PO Box 708
Adams Basin, NY 14410-0708
Visit us at www.thewildrosepress.com

Publishing History
First Crimson Rose Edition, 2012
Print ISBN 978-1-62830-158-8
Digital ISBN 978-1-61217-354-2

Published in the United States of America

As Stacey began to peel off the towel and reach for the robe, she heard a click. She grabbed for the robe, struggling with it while still holding onto the towel as the door opened. Why hadn't Peg knocked?

But it wasn't Peg who peered at her, accompanied by a sharp intake of breath.

"What... who... are... you?" Stacey gasped, attempting to clutch the robe and towel to her chest. Her shaking fingers slipped and she dropped both.

"A better question is who the hell are you and what are you doing in my bedroom?"

"Your...your bedroom?" Her gaze traveled wildly around the room.

The man didn't answer. He jerked back and slammed the door. "Can you please put your clothes on?"

Her breath exploded in quick pants. What was going on? Peg directed her to go to the top of the stairs, take a left and go to the first bedroom. Stacey held up her hands and studied them like a map. Left formed an L. Oh, damn, she'd done it again!

And she knew who was behind those surprised blue eyes. Her new boss, Mack Warren.

Dedication

To my sister, Lillie, and brother, John,
who are always there when it counts.

Chapter One

"I need your help. You're the only one I can trust."

Helen's frightened voice haunted Stacey Moreno as she steered her car along a narrow road through a misty world of towering pines. The words appeared as a title tattooed over the mist that hung light as a shroud in front of her. It beckoned like a sign pulling her forward.

"Come... Please."

"I'm here, Helen," Stacey whispered as rain pelted her Honda. Big droplets splashed like tears on the windshield. She shivered despite the heat that poured from the car's vents. Yes, she was here—but it was too late, and she had only guilt to drive her forward.

Helen's phone plea for help two weeks ago was the last time she talked to her best friend. Two days later Helen was dead—suicide, according to police reports. Stacey didn't believe it for a minute. Helen Stanton embraced life. She wouldn't kill herself.

The rain shot down harder, becoming bullets on the roof, bursting against the windshield until she couldn't see. Stacey jerked her foot from the gas pedal and tapped the brakes, sending her car into a spin. She fought for control and regained it after a heart stopping swerve.

"This is crazy. I should go home," she muttered.

No!

She'd let Helen down once. She couldn't do it again. Her thoughts drifted to Kendra, the cartoon character she created for sketching. *What would*

Kendra do? Since Kendra was based on Helen, the bottom line was *what would Helen do?* Press forward, that's what.

Stacey had come to Washington's San Juan Islands wanting to find out more about where and how Helen died. Her first stop on Evergreen Island was the general store Helen once described to her. The last thing she expected to find as she wandered the store looking for snacks was a notice on the community bulletin board that was identical to the one Helen answered six months ago.

Wanted: Researcher and typist. Must be well organized and prepared to work long hours. Job is on an isolated island so room and board may be arranged.

Helen had loved her work at first, texting and emailing Stacey with glowing reports. She even admitted a growing crush on her handsome boss, Mack Warren. Then things changed... *Why?*

Stacey wanted answers and the ad promised the possibility of getting them. She knew what Kendra/Helen would do to uncover the truth. She'd go after the job and meet the mysterious Mr. Warren. She could envision the cartoon panels in her head as she punched in the phone number listed on the ad.

His sister, Peg, sounded pleasant enough when she agreed to have Stacey drive out for an interview. "You live on Evergreen Island?"

"I just came in on the ferry. I'm from Oregon."

"And you want to stay?" There was a half laugh on the other end of the line.

"The ad said something about room and board?"

"That can be arranged. We're about 20 minutes from town."

What had she been thinking? She'd left her mother's townhouse in Portland for this?

No! For Helen. But her imaginary cartoon panel

didn't include a rain soaked trip along a forest road so narrow it resembled a wet, green cave. Stacey glanced at the hastily scrawled instructions on how to get to Redfern Manor. She should almost be there.

She rounded a corner and the trees fell away to an open area. On the right side of the road sat a sprawling gray stone structure with an octagonal turret perched atop like a predator. Stacey skidded to a stop beside a stone sign that identified it as her destination. Redfern Manor resembled a gargoyle ready to pounce on cars coming around the corner. Two dark upper windows gave the top floors the ghastly appearance of a face with small black eyes. A tiled roof that sloped over a long veranda formed a red slash of a frowning mouth. Slanting eaves and a steeply pitched roof promised hiding places for vampires, werewolves and unknown creatures of the night.

"Holy cow!" What a setting for a Kendra adventure! But she wasn't Kendra. Or Helen. Perhaps meeting the Warrens was enough. She probably wouldn't get the job anyway. Drawing a deep breath, Stacey stepped on the gas to turn the car into the driveway. To her horror, the Honda sputtered and the engine died.

****

Stacey stepped reluctantly from the deep bathtub with a sigh and gripped a soft towel like a lifeline, pulling it snugly around her. She could have stayed in there for another half hour, wrapped in that wonderful scent of citrus and lime. Despite the hot bath, chills still rippled through her. Would she ever feel warm again? This sense of unwelcome iciness had overwhelmed her spirit when she first heard of Helen's death and refused to thaw.

Now she was only a few miles from the beach where Helen died. She'd managed to get Helen's old job and she was in the house where her friend lived her final days. She might even be in the very room where Helen spent her last night.

Stacey padded into the adjoining bedroom. The bulky walnut furniture was as stolid as the house and the heavy emerald drapes and matching bedspread on the king-sized bed were downright depressing. Lacy drapery blocked out any hint of daylight. She couldn't imagine her lively friend residing in this funeral parlor atmosphere. Helen loved bright places, not gothic inspired buildings with somber gray walls and Victorian décor. She belonged in a room painted red with black rugs and sleek chrome furnishings, not dark wood paneling and overstuffed furniture. While it suited Stacey better than her mother's delicate French Provincial, pink-themed townhouse, she still might ask if she could put up some Kendra drawings to liven up the drab environment.

What would Kendra do now?

"Get some clothes on," she muttered. Stacey glanced toward the bathroom and the clump of damp clothes that littered the marble floor.

When was her bag going to arrive? Stacey had given her car keys to Peg Warren, who in turn handed them to a rough looking, scrawny teen and ordered him to start the car or get it towed into the driveway. She'd also instructed him bring in Stacey's bag, and as though she suddenly noticed Stacey's shivering appearance, Peg suggested she come upstairs and take a hot shower. Stacey had opted for the luxurious tub instead.

Stacey paced around the room, stopping by the window to look for her car. Sure enough, the silver clunker was parked outside a long, low structure that must be the garage. At least it had gotten her here—250 miles from Portland to the Anacortes ferry landing north of Seattle. If she'd known it wouldn't get her home, she might have been more reticent about the trip.

But she had a job! Wait until she told her mother. She'd try calling her again, if she could get her cell phone to function. It worked fine in town when she called Peg, but showed no service now. No wonder Helen had trouble reaching her.

As Stacey turned, she spotted a robe. Forest green and soft to the touch, it rested on the back of a wing chair just outside the bathroom door. Peg must have left it for her. It would be more comfortable than prancing around in the towel until her bag arrived.

At least she could put on her underwear, since it was dry. She went into the bathroom, picked up her bra and panties from the towel rack and returned to the bedroom. As Stacey began to peel off the towel and reach for the robe, she heard a click. She grabbed for the robe, struggling with it while still holding onto the towel as the door opened. Why hadn't Peg knocked?

But it wasn't Peg who peered at her, accompanied by a sharp intake of breath.

"What...who...are...you?" Stacey gasped, attempting to clutch the robe and towel to her chest. Her shaking fingers slipped and she dropped both.

"A better question is who the hell are you and what are you doing in my bedroom?"

"Your...your bedroom?" Her gaze traveled wildly around the room.

The man didn't answer. He jerked back and slammed the door. "Can you please put your clothes on?"

Her breath exploded in quick pants. What was going on? Peg directed her to go to the top of the stairs, take a left and go to the first bedroom. Stacey held up her hands and studied them like a map. Left formed an L. Oh, damn, she'd done it again!

And she knew who was behind those surprised

blue eyes. Her new boss, Mack Warren. *Yikes!* Giving the room a second glance, Stacey realized how blind she'd been. Various masculine—and personal—objects leaped to her attention, a book on the bedside table beside black horn-rimmed glasses. Pictures on the bureau of a woman and boy. If she hadn't been so focused on Helen, she would have paid more attention.

Oh, rats!

What would Helen do? Easy answer—she wouldn't have gone in the wrong direction. Stacey was the dummy who'd never been able to tell her left from her right. She jerked on the robe, but even that reminded her of her mistake. The large garment wrapped around her like a drooping emerald curtain.

Oops.

A quick rap reminded her Mack Warren waited outside.

"I'm dressed," she called.

He opened the door and glanced in at her. His blue eyes reminded her of a bright June morning warmed by the summer sun. For the first time since she'd boarded the ferry, she felt warm. But heat came only from his gaze. His firm jaw was clamped tight, and his scowl could have frozen her. The jagged scar that slashed across his right eyebrow and upper cheek made him look fierce.

"When I said get dressed, I didn't mean put on *my* robe." He moved forward in a hesitant motion before dropping his head and running a hand through thick sandy hair.

"My bag hasn't arrived yet." As she spoke, Stacey recognized how lame that sounded. It probably was sitting in the right room. She tucked her damp hair behind her ear, though she would have preferred to remain hidden behind the thin curtain of her straight bangs. "I...got lost...see after

I talked to Peg…"

He held up a hand, to stop her rambling and jerked his head toward the door. "Your room is down the hall."

She gestured toward the bathroom. "My clothes…"

"Don't worry about them."

Stacey started for the door but stopped. This was off to a bad start, but she needed to explain. "My car died at the gate so I pushed it off the road…and…"

"That's your car blocking my garage door?"

Double, double rats!

"I'm sorry about this mess. I was all wet and Peg said to go to the first door on the left at the top of the stairs."

His brow furrowed as he tilted his head to the side. "This is on the right."

Embarrassment enveloped her and her face burned. "I…sometimes get directions confused." She held up her hands and attempted to explain her theory. "See, the left hand makes an L. Have you ever noticed that? But sometimes I forget to check…"

Mack Warren glared at her as though she was some sort of deranged nut case. "Will you just…" he gestured at her body.

"Sorry. I'll bring back your robe after it's washed…"

He lurched toward her and she jumped back as he leaned over. When he straightened, something pink and lacy dripped from his left hand.

"Oh," she said, grabbing her underwear, which she'd dropped along with the towel when he entered. Maybe it was time to shut up. Helen accused her of babbling when she got nervous. And she was beyond anxious! Holding her head down, Stacey rushed past him and out the door. What a fiasco! She knew what her mother would say: *"Stacey, you will never make it on your own.*"

But she had gotten Helen's job. Or maybe Peg felt sorry for the freezing creature she'd found shivering at the end of the drive pushing her car off the road. Peg had picked her up and they started the interview while driving toward the sprawling gray monstrosity.

A door opened in front of Stacey. A tall, thin woman stood framed in the doorway. "Miss Moreno?"

"Yes." Stacey waved at the hall. "I'm looking for my room."

"This is your room," the woman said, opening the door wider and gesturing for Stacey to enter. "Miz Warren asked me to prepare it. I'm Mrs. Delaney, the housekeeper."

Yep, she was housekeeper material all right, straight out of central casting. Of medium height, she wore a black cotton dress, as though she performed as Miss Danvers in *Rebecca* in her spare time. Her dark hair was streaked with gray and pinned on top of her head. Her eyes were small and dark and her pale face was lean, with a narrow nose and thin lips. She wore no makeup. Her sharp features and steady gaze reminded Stacey of a bird—perhaps a gray starling or a black crow. Stacey recalled that Helen once told her she did not trust the housekeeper.

"You'll be working for Mr. Warren?" Mrs. Delaney asked as Stacey stepped passed her into the room.

"Yes, I'm taking Helen Stanton's place."

The woman's thin lips pinched together in a disapproving twitch. "She killed herself, you know."

Stacey drew a deep breath to keep from an automatic response that Helen would never do such a thing. "Was this her room?"

The woman turned to a window and lifted a lacy curtain to reveal a pile of charred rubble behind the garage. "She didn't like staying here in the main house so they let her live in the old carriage house. That was a mistake. She burned it down."

Again, Stacey had to stop from protesting. This was new information. Helen never told her about living in a carriage house or that it burned down.

Mrs. Delaney pulled back from the window and straightened the curtain. "She had an argument with Mr. Warren. They say she set the house on fire just before she killed herself. Maybe she realized she had burned her bridges here."

A tremor shook Stacey and she licked her lips, trying to think of a response. "You didn't like her?"

"No one did." Mrs. Delaney walked to the door and stopped to look at Stacey, small eyes narrowed, prune-shaped face unforgiving. "Mr. Warren shoulda fired her after that first week. I told him so."

Stacey pressed her lips together and clenched her fingers into fists to keep from blurting an angry response. She couldn't make people angry on her first day. This woman's comments cemented her reason for being here. She needed to find out why these people turned against her friend. Helen had always been the friendly sort. What had happened here at Redfern Manor?

****

With nothing to do until dinner, Stacey settled in front of a delicate cherry wood writing desk with her sketch book. She opened it and sighed at the first picture. Done in charcoal it was a drawing of Helen and a self portrait of herself on a bench beside the Columbia River.

They'd sat side by side when she made the drawing, but she sketched it as though someone standing at the edge of the water had snapped their picture. Both were smiling, but the contrast between the two was startling. Helen had thick short onyx hair that feathered around her small oval face, while

Stacey's shoulder length curtain was thin and she'd used light gray lines to portray its mousey brown shade. Helen's dark eyes and pouty, exotic mouth appeared animated while Stacey's face showed an average nose, a small bow for a mouth and wide eyes in a delicately boned face. Even in charcoal, Helen looked real and vibrant, while Stacey portrayed a pale comparison as though a copying machine had lost its toner and her half of the sketch was a fading gray.

That was their final afternoon together after Helen had gotten her job on Evergreen Island. It was a bittersweet day, because while Stacey was pleased at her friend's good fortune, she was losing her roommate and her freedom. Having just lost her job, Stacey was moving back in with her mother. They stored their belongings in her mother's garage until three weeks ago when they moved them into a storage locker at her mother's demand. That weekend was the last time Stacey saw Helen. A week later, Helen made the frantic call that set the foundation for this journey.

"Stacey, I'm in trouble..." Static interrupted her shrill voice before it faded.

"Helen?" Concern filled Stacey at her friend's hint of panic. Helen didn't get scared.

"It's falling apart..."

"Hon, I can barely hear you. Can you call from a regular phone?" Stacey squirmed in her mother's uncomfortable chair, but Helen's tone was more disconcerting.

"...he figured it out... Please... I need help."

"Help?" Stacey choked back a laugh. From her? Unlike Helen who escaped scrapes through wit and charm, Stacey stumbled from disaster to disaster. She got fired from jobs and dumped by her boyfriend. Helen lived. Stacey survived through books, movies and Kendra cartoons.

"I…my backpack. Did you see it?…purple?"

"I thought you wanted it to go with your stuff. It went to the storage locker."

"I need it…"

"Shall I mail it? Or are you coming home again?"

"You must bring…need help…"

Stacey to the rescue? "Helen, I can't."

Helen didn't seem to hear. "Tomorrow, okay?"

"I can't get it by then."

"…afternoon ferry. I'll meet…"

"I'll have to find it and I can't go until tonight, but I'll mail it tomorrow."

"No…bring…"

Helen's words were cut off and Stacey saw the line was disconnected. She'd tried to call back but got no answer. When she went to get the backpack, she couldn't find it in the disorganized locker. She left a message and was continuing her search when Helen's dad called to say his daughter was dead.

Stacey still felt horrible about letting her friend down. So she was here now—for all the good it did. With a sigh, she turned the page and began a charcoal sketch of Redfern Manor. She drew the tilting lines of the roof and dark windows on the third floor. With a smile, she even outlined a couple of gargoyles. They belonged there. Satisfied with the gothic look, she turned the page.

Now what should she draw? Or who? The answer was simple—Mack Warren. As master, he fit the house perfectly—big and brooding. The gothic lord of old would have worn all black, and Mack had worn a thick black cable turtleneck sweater and dark brown corduroy jeans. Instead of dark hair and coloring, though, his light hair and tall stature gave him the appearance of a Nordic god. His face was chiseled and sharply lined, handsome in the traditional sense, except for those scars on the right side. But those scars added character—a Norse warrior perhaps instead of a god.

Stacey nodded and drew the angle of his strong jaw and the patrician lines of his nose and deep set eyes. Then she recalled the fire in his blue-eyed gaze. Even now it seemed to burn through the paper. If she could get her mother to send her painting supplies, she might try to match the color. She finished with the full lines of his lips, pursed in disapproval. Would he fire her for being an idiot?

With an impish smile she lengthened his hair and added a set of armor to her drawing. Yep, Norse warrior, just the sort Kendra might fight beside. Or take to bed? Her cheeks grew warm at the thought, recalling again those fiery blue eyes.

Thump!

The sound on the floor above her startled her. *What was that?* She waited to hear footsteps in the hall, but the floorboard creaked again and then there was silence.

She flipped back to her sketch of Redfern Manor. Was the damn place haunted? Should be if it wasn't. Pursing her lips, she drew the shadows of a couple of dark figures into the windows. She'd come looking to resolve the mystery of Helen's death and all the components of a good mystery were here— frightening house, sexy lord of the manor, peculiar housekeeper. And to solve the riddle?

Stacey? *Oh, brother!* She could almost hear Helen laughing.

Chapter Two

"Did you get settled in?" Mack asked as Stacey sat down at the dining room table. His gaze remained firmly on his lap as he placed a crisp white linen napkin across it, as though he didn't want to directly look at her. Could she blame him?

"Yes, Mrs. Warren helped me." She fought to keep from clearing her throat because her voice sounded high and raspy. Three hours had gone by since he discovered her in his room clad only in a towel. Stacey turned warm at the recollection and knew her face must glow a vivid shade of red.

Where was Peg? The long maple table in the dimly lit dining room was set for three at one end. Candles in silver candlesticks lit the center of the table and antique sideboards held polished silver pieces and crystal vases with flowers. She felt underdressed in her jeans, denim vest and cotton shirt. Mack had changed into a gray cashmere sweater over a forest green turtleneck and dark wool slacks.

Stacey turned her attention to the bowl of creamy soup in front of her. She took a small taste and nearly swooned. "Wow, this is great. This sure didn't come out of a can." Maybe there was something to be said for Mrs. Danvers-Delaney.

"I'm glad you like it. Mrs. D. makes everything from scratch." He lifted a spoonful of the thick soup to his mouth with his left hand.

Left handed? She started to make a comment about left-handed people and then stopped. Helen had filled her in on Mack Warren's background. He was writing a book, but in the past he'd worked as a television reporter in Los Angeles. He'd retired after being injured in an airplane crash that killed his wife and son. His wounds had been to his right side and were serious enough that he required an assistant to do much of his typing. Recalling his hesitant movements earlier, she realized he'd moved with a slight limp.

The door across from Stacey swung open and Peg swept through. Statuesque and elegant in a lime cashmere sweater and beige wool skirt, she sported a more pleasant disposition than her brother. Her blue eyes were soft and the laugh lines around her red lips were pronounced. Her short, ash blond hair curled in wisps around an oval, patrician face. She smiled at Stacey as she settled into her chair. "Well, dear, you're looking much better. The shower warmed you up?"

"Oh, yes," Stacey said and lowered her face, knowing she was probably beet red. She couldn't look at Mack. It would be great to turn that silly meeting into a joke, but she wasn't going to lead the discussion. Had he told Peg about their awkward encounter?

For a few minutes they ate in silence until Mack put down his spoon and turned to Stacey. "I hope you're ready to get started early tomorrow. I have a deadline next week and I don't want to miss it."

Before she could answer Mrs. Delaney walked through the door, balancing three dishes. She set them on the table and picked up the soup bowls. The scent of salmon and spices rose from the plate.

Stacey inhaled the fragrant scent. Heavenly. Much better than microwave dinners she got at her mother's house. She attempted a smile at Mack as she lifted a fork to her mouth. "I'm ready to start whenever you need me."

"Good. My last assistant..." He shook his head.

"Did Peg tell you about her?"

"I didn't feel that was necessary. Stacey had all the necessary credentials you wanted." Peg leaned forward and fired a fierce look at her brother.

While Stacey was curious about their thoughts of Helen, she didn't want to show too much interest the first night.

Mack ignored his sister, blue eyes zeroing in on Stacey like lasers. "What you need to know is that my last assistant claimed to be great at organization, but she wasn't. She assured me she was top notch at so many things that didn't turn out to be true. You didn't do that too, did you?"

The question confused her. "Do what?"

"Embellish your credentials? Everything you told Peg was honest?"

Stacey almost choked on a piece of salmon. "Of course! I wouldn't do that sort of thing. I'm not a liar." She wasn't, not really. Leaving out facts wasn't the same as fabricating.

Peg cleared her throat in a disapproving manner. "Mack, don't interrogate her. I dictated to her and she was fast and accurate, even though she was cold and wet and probably extremely uncomfortable."

"Just so you know what the job is," he said. "Did she tell you it also includes long hours?"

"Mack." His sister's tone carried another note of warning.

He twisted toward Peg. "What? There were times we worked 17 hours a day. I just want to make certain she's aware of that."

Stacey had never worked at anything for that long—couldn't even imagine it—but his words carried a challenge. She turned to him and tilted her chin up defiantly. "I can handle it."

Oh, rats, was she embellishing?

Peg rewarded her with a wink from across the

table. "I'm sure you can."

Stacey smiled in silent thanks and focused on her food as Mack and Peg fell into a discussion about hiring someone to clean up around the fire site. Neither mentioned Helen or the fire's cause.

Finally Peg got to her feet and gathered their plates. "I'm going upstairs. Goodnight, Stacey and welcome to Redfern Manor."

Seconds later Mrs. Delaney appeared with two pieces of a creamy pie and a teapot. She poured for both before disappearing again.

Stacey told herself she was being polite as she dug into the pie, but if she stayed long, she was going to gain weight. She tried not to gush over the heavenly taste of bananas and cream.

Mack took a couple of bites and cleared his throat. "Perhaps Peg told you about the scope of work, but I doubt she filled you in on the subject."

"No, she didn't."

"Lily Feeney." He spoke the words softly, like a prayer.

"Lily..." Stacey shook her head, not wanting to admit she had no idea who that was.

He didn't appear to notice, waving his left hand at the room as his voice grew animated. "She grew up in this house. Her great-grandfather built a railroad and her grandfather ran the business until his death. Or rather, he ran it into the ground. Her father's brothers and sisters sold off the remaining company assets, except for Redfern Manor. Her father took his considerable proceeds and lived a meaningless life in San Francisco, leaving Lily here with her grandmother. After the old woman died, the house was sold and Lily moved to Hollywood with dreams of becoming an actress. Unfortunately, the place destroyed her." He drew a deep breath, his gaze becoming remote as though he'd retreated into another world.

"She was murdered," Stacey finished. When he mentioned Hollywood, she finally remembered that she had heard the name. "By a serial killer? Is that who you're writing about?"

His focus returned and he jerked around toward her. "Kevin Greenlee? Why would I write about him? His story has been told numerous times. He sat on death row for years. I covered his appeals and interviewed him before he was executed five years ago. He was never convicted of killing Lily and in our final interview he claimed she wasn't one of his victims."

Stacey almost choked on her pie. "You think he didn't do it? Is that what your book is about?"

The blue eyes suddenly lit up, sparkling like a sunlit ocean. "What do you think, Stacey?"

The force of his gaze hit her like a wave splashing over her and she almost dropped her fork. "What?"

His eyes danced, filling with delicious promise, and her stomach tingled inside. She dropped her head, lowering her field of vision to the remnants of her desert, but she couldn't keep it there for long. His voice was low when he spoke, almost hypnotic, drawing her back to him.

"Do we leave the ending as a mystery? See, that ugly end isn't my story. I'm looking for the answers behind Lily Feeney the woman, not the actress. I'm looking at what drove her to seek the golden dream that left her dead at the hands of a monster. That's what makes her story so tragic. The other victims were runaways and prostitutes. Lily had money and breeding and came from a legendary Northwest family. Was she really one of his victims? Or a casualty of the Hollywood dream machine? Maybe I'll leave it with that question."

He nodded at her as though they shared a big secret. As he turned toward her she noticed another series of scars that ran under his right jaw line. Despite that, with his full lips turned up in a smile and his eyes dancing like brilliant blue sapphires, she'd never seen anyone so handsome. Her breath caught as that crazy tingling in her stomach turned her insides to mush. She jerked her head down again as her heart skipped and began a crazy, erratic beating. *What was happening here?*

He didn't seem to notice her strange reaction. His voice took on an animated timbre as he continued. "When I was reporting on the Greenlee case, her story leaped out at me. What turned Lily into such a little girl lost? Doesn't that grab your interest?"

Stacey nodded but her enthusiasm was feigned. Didn't countless girls go west harboring the dream of Hollywood? Had Helen grown bored with the concept? What had changed her mind about being here? She'd been so enthusiastic when she took the job but sounded spooked at the end. Maybe Redfern Manor frightened her and made her want to live in the carriage house.

"Are you doing anything on her life here? Before she went to Hollywood? What about her life in this house? Or this house itself?" Stacey asked.

He looked puzzled. "What about it?"

"Well, like if the place is haunted?"

He laughed sharply and studied her until she felt warmth rise in her cheeks. "If I say yes, will you quit?"

She met his gaze as Kendra or Helen would. "I stand by my obligations. I'm ready to work."

"Good. But no, the house isn't haunted. Have you seen something?"

"I heard a noise, up on the third floor." She felt stupid the instant the words left her lips, as the light disappeared from his eyes.

"I doubt that. There's no one up there now. That

was Lily's area. I'll give you a tour tomorrow so we can look at her room."

Stacey attempted a half hearted shrug. "I guess it was just a creaking."

"Old houses do that," he said in a stern voice, carefully folding his napkin and placing it on the table. "Now, perhaps you should start tonight with some homework. I'll give you publicity pamphlets for Redfern Manor. The previous owners ran this place as a bed and breakfast and gave them to all the guests. They have information about the Feeney family and the house. That way if you run into any ghosts, you'll know who they are."

Her gulp was audible and for the first time since she'd met him, Mack Warren laughed. The husky sound filled the room and stirred that crazy awareness within her again.

He reached out toward her in a soothing motion and she looked at the large hand with its long fingers...and a wedding band. Hadn't his wife been killed in the plane crash?

"Don't worry, Stacey. No one has seen ghosts, but Lily's presence is here. I can feel it." He looked up at the carved wooden ceiling and nodded. "It's why I bought this place."

****

Stacey thought about Mack's comments as she walked downstairs for her first day of work. She'd locked herself in the previous night to read the pamphlets. At least her bathroom was adjoining— one of the upgrades made when Redfern Manor was a bed and breakfast. Too bad they hadn't updated the green floral wallpaper or faded blue carpets.

She tugged at her sweater, bringing it down over the top of her jeans, wishing she had packed more clothing. Since she'd intended on being gone for only two days, she'd included only a few casual clothes. Hopefully her mother would send more. Not that her mother was happy with her decision to remain on Evergreen Island. Stacey had reached her after dinner to give her the news about her job.

"That's the craziest thing I've ever heard," her mother scolded. "You better tell them you've had second thoughts and come home."

"For the past few months, you've been saying I needed to find work, Mom."

"Here in Portland. What kind of job is it?"

It was at that minute that Stacey decided it was best not to tell her it was Helen's old job. "Clerical," she said instead. "Typing, filing. Like what I was doing for that shipping company."

"Where will you live?"

"I found a place…"

"Phil called yesterday. You should make up with him. I always thought the two of you belonged together."

"He broke up with me," Stacey reminded her.

"Hmph, it sounds like he wants you back. Call him, sweetie."

She ignored the plea. "Can you please send some of my good clothes? I need to look professional. My black slacks and wool skirts? Some sweaters?"

Her mother sighed. "I suppose. How can I reach you?"

"My cell works most of the time, and I'll get a post office box tomorrow and call back with the number." Giving her mother the address of Redfern Manor was not a good idea. She was likely to show up to demand Stacey return home. But her mother's townhouse wasn't really home! She was twenty-five years old. She needed her own place. Maybe she could save enough from this job to get out on her own again.

For now, Redfern Manor was a preferable place to live, even if its décor was somewhere between old Victorian aunt and funeral parlor. Reaching the bottom step Stacey slowed as her footsteps clicked on the wooden parquet floor. How long would it take before she could find her way around? Maps in the pamphlets had helped. She knew the center staircase that rose from the entryway split the house into a front and back on the second floor. Mack's bedroom door was in the front with a door to the third floor stairs across from it. The back portion held Peg's room, the room Stacey occupied and another bedroom at the end of the hall. The third floor held more bedrooms plus a large area, which was once the playroom for the Feeney children.

Why did Mack and his sister want to live in this monstrosity? Built in the late 1800s, the house was more museum piece than home. The exterior walls and nearby fences were constructed of gray stone from a nearby quarry, according to what she'd read. The Feeney family had shipped in a variety of woods from around the world for the interior.

Stacey crossed toward the door which the map labeled the parlor. She was supposed to meet Mack at 8:30, five minutes from now. She paused, staring at the oak door with its polished brass door knob. Was he already inside?

An antique table with a crystal vase sat across from the door. The vase held a colorful bouquet of flowers. She touched one with the tip of her finger, surprised to discover they were real.

"You shouldn't touch things."

She jumped and whirled around to find a young man watching her from the end of the hall. Lank black hair fell to his shoulders. Thin and wiry, he moved toward her with the grace of a feral cat, despite heavy black boots. His brown eyes were dull, his skin very white. Earrings lined both ears and tattoos were scattered along his arms like spiders below a tight black t-shirt. She recognized him as the youth Peg had ordered to move her car.

"They'll fire you if you break any thing," he added.

Stacey jammed her hands in her pockets. "You're Joe, right? Thanks for moving my car. I'm Stacey Moreno. I just got hired."

"I know. My mom's the housekeeper and does the cooking. You seen her? She's not in the kitchen."

"I saw her at breakfast. Her biscuits were heavenly." She smiled at the lanky boy. "She's a great cook."

His unfriendly expression didn't change. "Have you seen Del?"

"Who's Del?"

"Old man trouble. Supposed to fix things, but all I see him do is cause problems." He didn't wait for a reply. He slinked past her and out the front door.

What an odd bunch. Stacey approached the parlor door and pushed it open. She found Mack sitting behind an antique wooden desk, but he didn't look up. He was gazing at a small instrument in his right hand while his left thumb worked frantically. Beside him, a light- haired boy watched, eyes transfixed.

"Oh, no," the boy cried. "He got you. That's your last shot."

Mack laughed. The pleasant sound sent a buzz through her system. She liked hearing the gentle rumble of his laughter.

"Darn!" Mack said, shaking his head. He glanced up, saw Stacey and handed the boy the instrument. "I'll get him next time, Kenny."

"That's still not as many total points as I have."

"Bring it next time. I can do better." Mack mussed his hair and pointed at the door. "Now get going, buddy. I have to work."

"I better find Joe," the boy said with a glum expression.

"He just went out the front door, looking for his

mom," Stacey offered. "Hi, I'm Stacey Moreno."

"This is Kenny Delaney." Mack placed a hand on the boy's striped t-shirt. "He's a whiz at computer games, but I can beat him sometimes." He smiled as the boy turned and raced out the door.

Stacey had not moved beyond the entryway and Mack waved her inside. "Come in. Are you always this timid?"

How could he think that after their initial meeting? Her face burned at the thought as she stepped toward him. "I've been told I talk too much when I get nervous." She grimaced at the silly sound of her words. When would she stop sounding like such a goofball?

"Are you finding your way around?"

"Yes. This is quite a house." She glanced around the room. It wasn't as big as the room across the hall where Peg had interviewed her. The pamphlet called it a parlor, but the room had been converted to an office. Tall mahogany bookcases dominated the area behind Mack's desk and the other inside wall was lined with filing cabinets and stacks of sagging cardboard boxes. Antique wing chairs that straddled the edges of a royal blue and gold rug were piled with manila folders. Even the space under tall windows that faced the side and front verandas held more boxes. The only neat area was a small writing desk near the front windows. It held a laptop and had a secretary chair beside it.

"This is where we'll be working," he said, gesturing around the room.

She nodded, stifling her true feelings. Were those boxes and folders what she was supposed to organize? How long would that take?

"That's your desk and laptop, but the computer is not to leave this room. It's brand new, state of the art, but it has no games and Peg and I have the only internet connections in our rooms. Don't think you're free to remove it from that spot or go online with it."

She walked toward the desk with a lump in her throat. His negative warnings didn't matter. She was more thrilled with the whole idea. A new job! Her own workstation! She realized he was waiting for her to answer him. "Don't worry, I wouldn't do that."

His lips drew together in a tight straight line. "That's what your predecessor said, but her computer ended up as a smoking piece of plastic because she took it to her room."

Stacey winced. Naturally Helen would assume she could take work supplies anywhere. At least his comments explained why Helen's email correspondence was so erratic.

Behind her, he continued. "We'll be working in here and nothing is ever to leave this room, understand?"

After his playful attitude with the boy, he sounded so stern Stacey couldn't help but attempt to lighten up the conversation. "So where is the ghost? It didn't visit me last night."

His look was hard, but slowly it dissolved as a smile creased his features and the blue eyes lit up. "I hope I didn't scare you. Sometimes I can't help myself."

Her breath caught. Such a pleasant smile and such captivating eyes. Stacey felt the blood rush to her face. She touched her hand to her warm cheek, as though that might hide the flush she knew was spreading.

"Let's get started," he said, shoving aside folders on a visitor chair beside his desk.

He gestured for her to sit down. "Tell me how much you know about Lily."

After their talk, she'd tried to remember her, but only came up with one thing. "She was on a TV sitcom for a couple of years, playing an older sister."

"Right! She had two movie parts plus some television credits. What about her death?"

"Her body was found on a hillside in Hollywood."

His nod was approving. "Her body was dismembered and positioned like all of Greenlee's killings. His other victims were prostitutes or runaways who frequented Hollywood Boulevard, and witnesses described a man resembling him near the spot where Lily's body was found. Police didn't have enough evidence to try him for her murder, but because it was so similar, she's considered one of his victims."

"Why didn't he protest until that final interview? He admitted killing the others, right?"

"He said he preferred the title Hollywood Stalker to the Hooker Killer, which was what he'd been dubbed before Lily. He claimed her death was a copycat, but police closed her case when he was arrested. During the appeals process, I became friends with the LA detective who took the original call on Lily's case. Name of John Scotti. He also had doubts about Greenlee. John had to turn the case over to the Stalker task force so he never fully investigated it, but he said my interview with Greenlee convinced him he was right." He paused and rubbed his hands together.

She was surprised to see he had some movement in his right hand and realized she was staring at him and again he was waiting for her to answer. "How did you get involved?"

"John and I got to talking when I started my research on Lily. He was retired too, so we decided to pursue it together. I gathered information on her personal life and he went through the old police records. He was hoping the book would get some interest and get the case re-opened. Unfortunately he died of a heart attack before we got very far."

Her gaze traveled to the sagging piles of boxes.

"All of this came from one murder case?"

He blew out air in a heavy sigh. "That's the problem. These files are from all his cases. His wife said he wanted me to have them. I might someday write a book about John so eventually I will need them sorted. For now I want you to look through the files and separate any Feeney information. John wasn't organized so notes could be anywhere. My former assistant went through those files." He pointed at two open boxes containing folders beside her desk.

That was all Helen had accomplished in six months? This job could go on forever! Stacey fought to hide her dismay, but he didn't appear to notice.

"If Helen found information on Lily, she was supposed to date it and put it into a separate file. Instead she decided to also type up John's written notes on Lily. She claimed she was creating a timeline around the investigation, but now the notes she did find are missing. Of course the timeline she claimed to be creating and all her typed information was destroyed when her computer burned. She'd promised to keep everything on a flash drive for me, but I've never found it—if she even did it."

Mack sighed and she could feel the vibration of his frustration. The fire had taken a toll on his work, and he probably blamed Helen for the loss since she had taken the computer.

Stacey attempted a smile. "If you're worried about trusting me..."

His eyes shot to her, blue spheres, as cold as ice. "I don't trust anyone. The sooner you learn that, the better we'll get along."

Stacey licked her dry lips, uncertain what to say. "Why...why wouldn't you trust me?"

His gaze pinned her to the back of the chair, blazing with something she couldn't define. "I spent years as a journalist. I figure everyone has something to hide."

Her heart skipped. She felt as though he could see into her brain and discover her connection to Helen.

Then a corner of his lips twitched into a smile. "But then, you're probably the only person in the world who couldn't hide anything. Your face is like reading a lie detector readout. It turns bright red every time you get flustered."

Stacey brushed her hand across her cheek. It was burning right now, which meant it was probably the color of a valentine.

"I'm sorry if I sound like an evil tyrant," he continued, his face softening. "Peg had to fire my first assistant and the second just left. Now this thing with Helen Stanton..."

There had been other assistants before Helen? "Yikes, and you've hired me?"

"What does that mean?"

She wiggled her nose, making a face. "I guess that's my secret. Mom calls me a jinx. My first employer was shut down by the city. My second job lasted three months before I got laid off and my last employer closed after 93 years in business."

His gaze grew so intense that for an instant she feared he might fire her on the spot. Then he inhaled sharply and lurched to his feet. Favoring his right leg, he limped toward the front windows that looked out on the veranda. "As long as you do your work, you'll be fine. Since I'm paying you above normal wages I expect you to work hard and put in long hours."

"No problem. But I'll need some time off..."

He ran his hand through his hair in an abrupt gesture of dismay as she rushed to explain.

"I didn't know I'd get this job...so I need to go into town for...well...personal things. And I've asked my mother to send more clothes so I'll need to pick

them up tomorrow. Plus, my car needs to be fixed."
She stopped. She was rambling.

"Have Del look at your car. I've lost so much
time due to the fire and this death..." He sounded so
uncaring. Was that really the way he was? No. She
remembered him with the boy, Kenny. And he wore
his wedding ring. He must still love his wife.

Before she could reply, Mack held up his hand.
"Okay. Take the time you need. Let's get started. I'm
going to give you a combination of dictation and
written notes. One warning—my writing is awful
since I'm learning to use my left hand."

"You haven't tried typing with your left hand or
the software that does dictation?"

"If I wanted to do that, I wouldn't need you,
would I?"

Stupid, stupid. It wasn't her place to question
his motives. And it wasn't like she was worried
about the work. She'd always been a fast typist. As
for organizing the boxes, heck, Helen once teased her
that she was a librarian at heart.

"I'm sorry. That was uncalled for. I use dictation
because one-handed typing slows my thinking
process, and I found too many mistakes with voice
software. Now, how about a test?"

"A test?" Her throat constricted as her breathing
quickened in panic. *Uh Oh!*

"Tell me what you found out about the house?"

Stacey felt her body relax in relief. Finally
something she knew! She began reciting the facts
from the brochures. "The room across the hall was
the drawing room and there was a room behind it
that was a gentleman's club room or library but now
it's one big space?"

A smile tipped the corner of his mouth as he
nodded at her. "The previous owners knocked out
the walls to make it a lounge for their guests. They
removed the bookcases, which we installed here and

upstairs in my personal study. I like the old way better, and I may have the original walls reconstructed. They modernized the interior, but we're debating how to regain Redfern Manor's former charm. Peg's scouring antique shops and we found some of the old furnishings in storage, which is why the house has a split personality at the moment."

"I'll bet that screws with the ghosts' psyches."

His full lips pressed together and for an instant Stacey feared she'd angered him.

He rolled his eyes and chuckled. "I think you're obsessed with ghosts. Come on, let's go look at Lily's room."

Chapter Three

Stacey climbed the stairs to the third floor in front of Mack, aware of his halting progress due to his bad right leg. She stepped onto the landing and gave a low whistle. Here the house's split personality was in full view. A threadbare strip of rug ran the length of the hall though the walls were painted a cheery yellow. Through one door she could see blond furniture that looked straight out of a 50s movie set. She started to turn back toward Mack, but suddenly sensed movement at the back of the house where a shaft of sunlight spotlighted an antique rocker. Was it moving? No. But as she stared at it, she thought she glimpsed a shadow flutter in the light.

Was someone up here? Hadn't Mack unlocked the door to the stairs from a key ring in his pocket? She started to ask him, but stopped. No use continuing to push that ghost scenario.

"This was Lily's room." He pointed toward the room with the dated furniture.

She stepped to the doorway to gaze inside. A bedside table with a square lamp sat beside a twin bed with a faded quilt on top. The dresser was low and long with old movie magazines spread out on top. The large mirror had the name "Lily" written in red nail polish along one lower edge.

"This is her old furniture," he said, touching the dresser with a long finger. "According to her cousins she bought it at a second hand store because it reminded her of Marilyn Monroe. We also found some of her belongings in a trunk in the coach house."

Stacey turned away to hide her grimace. What a sad tribute to the girl who wanted to go to Hollywood. The room was like a museum display.

There wasn't much else to see. The back end of the house contained two empty bedrooms with modern bathrooms. Then he opened the door to a long room that extended the width of the house. The pamphlet labeled it the playroom and it showed its age. The wood paneled walls were badly scuffed and one section appeared to be defaced with childish carvings. An archway led into the octagonal turret and Stacey gasped in awe. The day was clear and through the windows she could see neighboring islands and beyond them, all the way to the Olympic Mountains on the western Washington Peninsula. Her fingers itched for her pencils and a sketchpad. Heck, she'd call her mother for her painting supplies.

Mack didn't appear to notice her reaction. "My study is just below this room. On mornings when I don't come down to the parlor, that's where I'll be."

"Admiring the view?" she teased.

He turned to her, and she wished she'd kept her mouth shut. His handsome face might have been carved in granite. "I'll tell you this once. Don't interrupt me when I'm in there. That room is off limits."

She lowered her head. Was he telling her that because he was worried she'd turn up naked in his room again? Her face flamed. "What if I need to reach you?"

"I have an intercom set up between my office and the parlor."

"What about up here, can I come...?"

He was already shaking his head, much to her dismay. "The doors to the stairs are kept locked. This was Lily's area. I want to keep it that way for now."

He stepped toward the wood paneled wall with its engravings. A long finger ran over one of the words, and as she approached, Stacey realized the carvings were actually names. "Lily" was carved in script letters. A shiver ran down Stacey's spine as he traced it as though touching a sacred object.

"Wow," she said without thinking. "Can you imagine her up here by herself in this huge old house with just her grandmother for company?" She stared out the window, at the mountains in the distance. "Think about what she must have thought when she saw those peaks in the distance and the ferry boats crossing the water. And all she wanted was to get to Hollywood."

"Yes," he said in a low, urgent voice. "You're exactly right. Can you identify with that? With how Lily might have felt, wanting to get out on her own? To get away?"

Stacey hadn't thought about it before, but in a way she was like that too. All she wanted was an opportunity to succeed on her own, but his hushed voice was giving her chills.

"Well, I mean, I have my mother and my life in Portland, and friends...but..." she stopped. She had no idea what else she wanted to say and he was staring at her like she was some sort of prophet.

The spell seemed to break and he turned away. "You might as well go down and get started on those files by the desk," he said, running his finger over the carved name again.

"I thought Helen Stanton already did them."

"They were sorted, but I want to make certain that Helen didn't misfile the Feeney information." His voice left unspoken that he didn't trust Helen's work. "I'd like you to give them a quick check. Let me know if you find anything or if you run across the missing flash drive. I'll be in my office."

She hopped down the stairs, eager to get away

from his odd behavior and ready to get started on the boxes of files. As she entered the parlor/office, she spied the intercom on her desk. She pushed down the "talk" button. "Hello?"

"Yes?" His voice sounded all business and she wrinkled her nose. Did he think she was a dummy for trying it?

"I wanted to see if it worked."

His quick chuckle sent a rush of warmth through her. "I see. Call me if you have questions."

"Yes, sir." She made a face at the intercom. His message was clear: *"Don't call just to chat."*

"By the way, call me Mack. Sir and Mr. Warren make me feel like an old man."

"Yes...Mack." She decided she liked the way his name sounded on her tongue as she clicked off the intercom.

With a sigh, Stacey began her work by pulling a pile of folders from the box. She stared at the top folder as a tear sprang to her eye. A date and the name "Carlisle," was written on a green sticky note in Helen's familiar handwriting. Stacey touched the words as though they might provide a connection to her friend.

"Helen," she whispered. She looked around the room made gloomy by the heavy drapes, thick lace curtains and veranda that held back the sun. No wonder Helen might have grown depressed— working in this somber atmosphere for a boss obsessed with a ghost in a house that had lost its character. As though Kendra poked her in the side with a spear she straightened up. She couldn't afford to let this depressing place get her down. She'd finish the job Helen started and maybe find out why her friend had died.

****

"Mr. Hamilton? Del?" Stacey called, stepping into the greenhouse.

33

A slim man in a plaid flannel shirt stepped out from behind a row of plants. He rubbed his hands on green stained jeans.

"You lookin' for me?"

"Yes. I'm Stacey Moreno."

His dull brown eyes flicked over her below his blue watch cap. A growth of stubble peppered his narrow cheeks. "Mary told me. You're takin' over for that dead girl, huh?"

"Yes. Mack told me I should ask you to look at my car."

"What's wrong with it?"

He showed little interest in her response before finally nodding. "Guess I can take a look. Is it that silver Honda in the driveway?"

"Yes."

He nodded and turned his back to her and went back to digging up a plant from a bed of flowers.

Stacey cleared her throat. "I don't mean to be rude, but could you look at it this morning? Mr. Warren gave me the afternoon off because he had to meet a friend at the ferry. I want to go into town to run errands, and I don't want to get stranded..."

His head jerked up and his small eyes studied her. He shoved the spade down on the counter. "Guess I don't have much choice, huh? Mr. Warren wants it done? Guess you're gonna be like that other girl, thinkin' you can order me around? I work for them, not you."

She held up her hands. "I'm sorry! If you can't look at it today, I understand."

He wiped his hands on a dirty towel that dangled from a pocket. "I'll do it now. Come back in an hour."

She glanced around, hoping to repair the broken good will. "I guess you grow all the flowers I've seen in the house? They're absolutely gorgeous. You must have a beautiful garden around here."

"Good enough."

"Anything like a formal garden? Some place I could walk while you work on the car?"

"No garden. And if you go off gallivantin' around, you gotta be careful of the quarry." He leaned his head to the side as though providing a direction. "It's the quarry where they dug up the stone that built this place."

"You mean like Buchart Gardens in Victoria?" What a great place that would be to draw!

He just stared at her. "This quarry is not that big and it's deep and full of water. Mainly it's a hazard."

"I'll be careful."

"I mean it. I told that other girl to stay away from the quarry but then she goes over to the other side and look what happened."

She tried to keep any emotion from showing. "Where...did she die?"

He cocked his head in the opposite direction, toward where she had come from the ferry. "A few miles the other side of town. It's called Three Mile Walk, a path at the edge of a bluff. Guess she jumped."

Stacey examined a pink rose, pretending indifference. Maybe once her car was running she would drive to the location.

"I don't know what her problem was," the man added. "Seemed normal at first. I guess this place just plain wore her down."

"That house is kind of depressing. Your flowers are the only bright spots."

He grunted. "Got nothin' to do with the flowers. It's the people. That Peg, always asking for things. Wants fresh flowers every day, but now she's takin' over half the greenhouse to turn into a studio. Like she'll use it. And Warren. Don't have time for no one. Made me build him a gym and don't use it. Just sits up there with his damn papers."

She sympathized with the man's views, but gave no indication she agreed. "I'm going for a walk. I'll be back in an hour."

"Okay, but if you go into the woods, stick to the right. Away from the quarry."

She left the garage uncertain where to walk. She could barely find her way around the house, but she wanted to be outside. She felt like she had been cooped up too long—first in her mother's townhouse in Portland and then here. She didn't want to make staying inside a habit.

Walking past the garage, Stacey winced as she saw the blackened area where the coach house once stood. Three fir trees sheltered one end. A shiver ran through her and she skirted the area. Behind the house she found a flagstone patio with white wicker furniture and a stainless steel grill. None of it looked used.

Stacey kept walking until she reached a path that led into the dense thicket of trees. The lush forest promised possible locations for a Kendra adventure. Silence descended on her as she stepped under the tent of towering trees. The foliage was so dense she couldn't see the sky. The only sound was the crackle of pine needles under her feet and even that grew muffled by a thick layer of leaves and moss. It wasn't raining but droplets of water fell from large emerald leaves. Her breath caught. This was beautiful. It was like being in another world.

Forgetting Del's warning, she pressed forward. This might be her only chance to explore. Once Mack finished with his friend, she might not get time off. He was probably gone by now. The quiet gave her the chance to think about Helen again. Why did people at Redfern Manor view her in such a negative fashion? No wonder they all believed she'd committed suicide. Could Stacey show them differently? And if Helen hadn't killed herself, how had she died? Had she fallen by accident?

Stacey could see the possibility. She had to step carefully, even along the path. Low branches shot out over the path and tree roots extended above the ground like long green veins. Uprooted trees sometimes covered the path. Even as she considered her footing, she caught her ankle on a vine and nearly tripped. She took another step and stopped. Spread out before her was a steep drop. Across from her were the sheer walls of the quarry.

Dizziness rocked her and Stacey drew back, knees shaking. She'd almost fallen in. If she'd tripped or taken two more steps forward... Hadn't Del said to go right? She held up her hands, studied them and shook her head. Naturally she'd gone to the left.

She turned and her foot caught on the roots again. Stumbling, Stacey cried out and the sound seemed to reverberate around her and echo in the quarry. She staggered toward the edge of the bank, propelled by her forward motion and she knew any second her feet would touch air. She reached out, trying to break her fall, and this time she connected. A sturdy hand grasped hers and pulled her back from the edge of the quarry.

"What the hell are you doing?"

She looked up into the startled eyes of Mack Warren. "I...fell..."

He scooped her up like a sack of flour, and she sagged against him, her body trembling. As he put her down, she leaned toward him, grasping him tightly around the neck.

"It's okay," he said in a soft voice.

Stacey was aware of the warmth of his large body as she pressed against him. He smelled clean and masculine and she recognized the lime scent from his bath soap that she'd used the first day.

Perhaps it was that smell, but she found herself drawn to him and was tempted to lean her cheek on his sturdy shoulder.

"Are you all right?" he asked, brushing her hair from her face. "What happened?"

She pointed down at the tangled roots. "I tripped."

His warm breath teased her cheek and she could feel his heart thudding through the hand she rested on his chest. As though he noticed their proximity and his overly familiar touch on her hair, he pulled back.

"What are you doing out here?" he asked, his voice taking on a gruff timbre.

"Taking a walk."

His lips drew into a straight disapproving line. "This isn't a good direction to come."

Breaking twigs crackled and Del Hamilton appeared. "I heard someone yell."

"She almost fell into the quarry."

"I told you to be careful," Del grumbled, eyes skewering Stacey.

Wonderful! What would Mack think of her now? "I'm fine," she protested.

Mack turned to Del and waved at the path. "Didn't there used to be a sign posted about the quarry?"

Del stretched his neck to look beyond them, and a surprised look crossed his face. "I had a board nailed to that tree. It musta fallen down or someone took it off."

"Well, put it back," Mack ordered. "Now. I don't want someone falling in and suing me because the quarry wasn't marked."

Del nodded, thin shoulders drooping and Stacey couldn't help but jump to his defense. "He...did tell me to stay to the right." She held up her hands and wiggled her left thumb. "I...um...got lost..."

Mack's cold stare was like hitting a hard blue wall. There was no doubting what he thought of her this time. Shaking his head and jamming his hands in his pockets, he turned away without saying a word.

Stacey approached Del and touched his arm lightly. "I'm sorry, Del. I should have listened when you warned me not to come into the woods."

A muscle in Del's stubbled jaw jumped in irritation. He gave her a brisk nod and stomped back along the path.

Mack came up behind her and took her arm. The touch on the elbow of her sweater was like a jolt of electricity. "Let's go back."

"Thank you for saving me..." she began.

He looked down at her, something unreadable in those bottomless sapphire eyes. "You need to be more careful. You're lucky I saw you come this way. I wanted to see if you needed a ride into town while Del works on your car. I can drop you off and Peg will bring you back when she goes in later."

Stacey couldn't face him, knowing how silly he must think she was. What made her think she could figure out the truth about Helen when she couldn't even tell her right from her left?

Chapter Four

The line of cars wound slowly away from the ferry dock into the narrow streets lined by two long blocks of clapboard structures. Despite a light rain, tourists meandered under umbrellas along wooden sidewalks outside gift shops, antique stores, and fishing outlets. A general store dominated a corner at the end of the first block. The next street began with a brightly lit coffee house. Beyond it was another series of shops and cafes before the town ended abruptly.

Stacey frowned as she peered into the crowded coffee shop. She'd finished her business at the post office, and that was where she was supposed to meet Peg in half an hour. She didn't relish the thought of jamming herself between the crowded tables, but she couldn't remain outside for long without an umbrella. She glanced up a side street and her breath caught. The Gull's Roost! Helen had posed for a picture outside the rustic log bar, telling Stacey this was where she spent free evenings.

It drew Stacey like a magnet. The interior smelled of stale beer and fried onions, and unlike the coffee house, the long room was nearly empty. Only one booth was occupied while two men slouched at one end of the bar. What did she hope to learn here? She didn't know. But like the job, it provided a connection to Helen.

"May I help you?" A hulking man with strands of gray hair combed over his balding head leaned across the bar.

"Um...coffee?" she stammered, shaking off her

wet jacket.

"Need a little nip in it?" he asked, slapping the bar with a napkin.

"Better not," she said with an apologetic smile. "I have to meet my boss later." She sat gingerly on the stool, examining the cavernous room. The walls were varnished logs, and the booths were made of polished pine. Blue vinyl cushions rested on the seats. Neon signs advertising various beers decorated the walls.

The bartender returned with a steaming mug. "Did you just get off the ferry?" he asked with a wide smile.

"I came in yesterday. How did you guess?"

His pudgy face wrinkled into a grin and his twinkling brown eyes were pleasant and open. "I know everyone who lives in town and everyone who has a vacation home. Name's Hap. Gonna be here long?"

"Maybe," she said, not certain how to answer.

"Where are you staying?" he asked.

As she sipped her hot coffee she could almost hear her mother's voice, echoing in her brain. *"Never tell a stranger too much about yourself."* Luckily she didn't have to answer.

"Hey, Hap, can we get some service down here?" The two patrons at the end of the bar simultaneously banged their empty glass mugs on the bar.

"Sorry," he said, waddling away. He stopped at the beer pumps in the center of the bar, pulled out two frosted mugs from a cooler and drew two frothy mugs of beer.

Stacey made a face at herself in the mirror behind the bar. How stupid was she for not coming up with a story before attempting this? Kendra/Helen would have a readymade spiel.

"Kinda quiet," one of the men said. He looked to

be in his late 30s, wiry, with a shaved head and narrow skull.

"Been quiet," Hap replied as he placed the mugs in front of the men.

"You hear any more about that girl?" the other man asked. He was burly and appeared to be all muscle beneath his gray t-shirt.

Stacey fought to hide her interest, though her skin prickled. Somehow she knew "that girl" was Helen.

"Nope," said Hap. "Nothing on the news."

"You'd think they'd say something even if it was suicide," the wiry man said.

"Suicide?" The word blurted from Stacey's lips before she could stop herself. Down the bar three pairs of eyes turned to her.

"Don't let them scare you." Hap waved a large hand. "We had a girl jump off a cliff not long ago."

Stacey's breathing grew shallow as a shiver ran through her. "I see."

Hap turned back to the men. "I'm gonna miss her. She livened up the place. Always had a smile, wanting to talk."

"You just liked the attention from a pretty young girl," the big man joked.

"Tease me all you want, Mike, but she was a pleasant kid."

"Why'd she kill herself then?" Mike replied.

"You're sure it was suicide?" Stacey asked. "I mean, did someone see her jump?"

"Nah," Mike said. "Kids found her body broken on the rocks."

The image jolted her. Stacey preferred to think of Helen visiting the bar, talking and laughing with Hap, not a mangled body at the bottom of a cliff.

"Damn Warrens probably drove her to it," the wiry man said. "That's a cold bunch."

Hap nodded. "Can you believe they were ready

to blame the fire at their place on her? Now I hear it was some damn electrical cord."

"Maybe you'll get a new friend," Mike said. "The sister came into the store the other day and put up a job notice on the bulletin board. It was in the paper too."

"See what I mean? Her body's barely in the ground." Hap shook his head in disapproval. "They're unfriendly. I hear the sister went through the antique shops being very particular and then demanded immediate delivery. The brother seldom comes to town. He's never been in once."

"He goes to that French café." Mike lifted his nose and adopted a false accent that drew laughs from the other men.

"Del don't mind 'em," the wiry man said. "Not that he's worth much. His no good cousin was down at the dock yesterday, looking for work. Just got out of state prison."

"Ray Gibson?" Hap asked. "He's back?"

"Yeah why? You got work to give him? He'll steal you blind."

"No, but that girl was lookin' for him the week before she died," Hap said.

The three men exchanged glances.

"Why?" Mike asked.

Hap shrugged. "I don't know. Don't think she found him, though."

Why would Helen look for a convict? Stacey was curious, but a quick glance at her watch told her it was time to go. She put money on the bar and waved goodbye at Hap.

The rain assaulted her as she stepped outside, and Stacey pulled her collar around her. In the distance the ferry was loading and Stacey was tempted to make a dash for it. She'd only been at Redfern Manor one day, but she sensed strange undercurrents. Even the townspeople seemed to confirm her misgivings. It was as though she'd wandered into a world where mist shrouded the truth, where shadowy figures took cover in that mist to hide their true intentions.

Kendra world for sure, but what could Stacey accomplish here? She shook off her negative thoughts. Why had Helen died here? More than ever, she wanted to find out.

****

Stacey sat at her desk, staring into the misty dawn, her only light coming from the narrow shaft of a desk lamp. Outside the towering fir trees beyond the garage resembled an invading army, poised for battle. She was drawing a sketch of the trees on either side of the house as opposing foes, facing off across the lawn.

She sketched Kendra in full armor leading one army. The other side had stolen the princess and she drew the abducted royal with Helen's face. Studying the trees for inspiration, she stopped, her fingers beginning to shake. Wait! Someone stood close to the fir trees beside the burned area. Who was it? The figure was too short to be Mack, too tall to be Del Hamilton and too big to be Peg. Joe maybe? What was he doing out there at five in the morning?

The figure shifted and she could have sworn he looked right at her. Panicked, she flipped off the desk light. Stacey sat in the darkness for a few minutes before approaching the window from the side. With her eyes adjusted to darkness she could make out the trees, but the figure was gone. Another one of those shadows concealed in the mist.

Putting away her drawings, she climbed back into bed, but couldn't fall asleep. Finally she headed for the shower and breakfast. At the bottom of the stairs, the sound of laughter drew her toward the dining room.

Mack stood as she entered. "Stacey, come in. I

want you to meet someone."

She stepped inside and stumbled, though she didn't know if it was the carpet that she misgauged or the slender man who sat at the table next to Peg Warren.

He stood and nodded at her. "Hello, I'm Mack's friend, Carlos Emory." His thick black hair was edged with streaks of gray and his lean dark face was wrinkled with lines that looked like he'd spent years in the sun. His wide smile displayed perfect, white teeth.

"Carlos stopped by on his way to Canada to cover a story," Mack explained. "He's my old photographer from Los Angeles. Stacey is my new assistant on the Feeney book."

She mumbled a hello to Carlos, aware of his insistent stare.

"Have we met before?" he asked.

Stacey lowered her head as fear tightened her muscles. They hadn't met, but she had seen him before. And he had probably seen her. The Warrens had not attended Helen's funeral, but Carlos had. She'd thought he was an old boss or teacher since he didn't stay long at the reception and Helen's immediate friends and family didn't appear to know him or who he was.

Did he recognize her? She'd worn a floppy black hat to the funeral to shelter her tear-stained face and covered her bloodshot eyes with dark glasses.

"I'm one of those people who looks...uh...generic," she said, summoning a smile.

His loud laugh rang around the room. "I see. Is the taskmaster keeping you busy?"

"We're just getting started," Mack said.

Peg rose and turned toward the door to the kitchen. "Would you like eggs, Stacey? I can have Mrs. D bring them in."

Not wanting to remain near Carlos, Stacey

started to follow Peg. "I can get them myself."

"No, no, stay and keep them company. I'm tired of their ghost stories."

"Ghost stories?" That was different. Curiosity swept her into a chair. She looked from Mack to Carlos but lowered her face as he regarded her with a gaze that seemed knowing.

"I accused Mack of being haunted by the ghost of Lily Feeney," he said.

"The house?" Her gaze shot to Mack.

To her surprise, his eyes shone with warmth. "She's convinced the house is haunted."

"Not really, but this morning I saw..." She stopped.

"Now you *saw* something?" Mack asked.

"Not a ghost. There was a man standing by the old coach house."

"Who?" He tipped his chin up toward Carlos. "Were you out there?"

Carlos held up his hands in a surrender motion. "Not me. What about that old guy?"

"Del won't be here for another half hour, and Joe didn't come today." Mack leaned toward Stacey. "Noises and now visions? If someone is haunting the place, you seem to be the only witness."

"Makes sense," Carlos added with a laugh. "The pretty young girl comes to the haunted house? Naturally the ghost would turn on her."

Her face burned. They were teasing her and she didn't like it. Her response erupted from deep inside her as though coming from someone else. "Maybe it's the ghost of Helen Stanton."

Both men jerked upright and they exchanged shocked glances. For a minute, neither spoke, and for a second she could almost hear Helen laughing with glee.

****

"Aren't you a cutie," Carlos said, throwing

46

himself into her chair and rolling it toward where Stacey kneeled on the floor, digging through boxes.

"Pardon me?" She refused to look up at him.

"Sweet, delicious, ripe, like a low hanging peach."

That was the second time he had made flirtatious comments and she drew back, knowing her cheeks must be turning bright red. "Please, Mr. Emory. I have work to do."

"Need help?"

"Do you know anything about Lily Feeney?" she asked, trying to sound sarcastic.

"I probably know more than Mack does. I was a young news photographer when those Stalker killings happened. I even covered a couple of them. I also shot Mack's interview with Kevin Greenlee. The day before he's scheduled to die, the guy claims he didn't kill Lily."

"Mack doesn't seem to believe he did."

"Does he? Or is he out to make a name for himself by writing a book that questions it?"

She jerked up. She hadn't considered that. "Really?"

His smile resembled a Cheshire cat grin. "What do you think?"

Stacey shook her head. He was teasing her again. She'd decided she didn't like Carlos, and it was more than her fear he might connect her to Helen. She wasn't practiced with men, but she knew his type. Carlos was out to impress any woman he met—even if they were years younger. He said he'd covered the Greenlee killings. That put him in his fifties.

"Did you know Helen Stanton very well?" she asked.

He put his hand to his chest. "What a leading question."

"Not at all. I'm going through the work she did.

47

From the looks of these files, she seems very organized, but Mack doesn't think so. Most of the people here didn't like her."

Carlos erupted with a boisterous laugh. "Of course not. Helen Stanton traveled to the beat of her own drummer. She didn't suffer BS very well, from Peg, Mrs. D or grumpy Del."

Stacey pressed her lips together to keep from smiling. He sounded as though he did know Helen well. "What about Mack?"

"Ah, what are you asking, young Stacey? If she and the boss had something going and maybe that was why she took the plunge?"

Could that be possible? Helen had been impressed by his good looks when she got the job, but she barely mentioned him that final weekend they were together. "What do you think?"

"It would have been all one-sided."

"Mack's still in love with his wife," she said, recalling his wedding band.

His grunt was a surprise. "Uh-uh. Mack's in love with lovely Lily."

"What?" Her head rose sharply in shock and she studied him.

His dark brown eyes were thoughtful, and his lean face had grown straight and serious. "He's obsessed with her. I wasn't kidding when I said he's haunted by her."

She thought about how Mack turned conversations toward Lily as well as his odd behavior when they visited her room. "I suppose haunted or obsessed, but in love with her?"

"Sure enough. She was Mack's type. That sweet, ethereal smile. Soft and delicate. Kinda like you."

Stacey felt her face grow warm and she turned away to huddle over the files. "You're teasing me."

"Just harmless flirting. Am I getting anywhere?"

"No. And if you don't mind, I need to finish this

work. I'm trying to find the Feeney information that Helen lost. Mack says it may be mixed in with these files."

He reached over and thumbed through a couple. "Having any luck?"

"Not so far, which is why I can't talk."

He shoved himself up from the chair. "All right. But if you decide I'm the man of your dreams, just say the word. I'm between wives right now. And before you say you're too young, my last wife was twenty-three."

She rolled her eyes, wanting to discourage him. "I have a boyfriend waiting at home." That wasn't entirely a lie. Phil had been her boyfriend until he decided she wasn't right for him. Her mother said he might want her back, so maybe he did still consider himself a boyfriend.

"Quick. What's his name?"

"Phil Bradley," she shot back without looking up. "We started dating in college."

"Well, good. We wouldn't want Mack to turn his attention on you, would we?"

"Why would he do that?" she asked, giving him a falsely sweet smile. "You said he's in love with Lily Feeney."

His dark eyes gazed at her so thoroughly they made her uncomfortable.

"Yes, but I'm starting to see you're more than just a sweet, fresh breath of air. Maybe you could make him get over that obsession."

She slammed a cover on one of the boxes. "It's a good thing I have Phil waiting at home."

****

The afternoon fog settled around her car like a blanket, but Stacey didn't stop. She drove past the ferry dock, in the opposite direction of Redfern Manor. She had come from the post office with her box of clothes, but she'd received more than just the package. Her mother had forwarded a letter from Helen. The lavender envelope rested on the seat beside her.

It was why she'd headed in this direction. The letter was like Helen calling to her. She was going to the spot where Helen died to read the letter. Del had said the place was called Three Mile Walk and she drove along the narrow road until she saw a sign. She turned into a gravel parking lot and grabbed the letter before getting out of her car.

Arrows pointed toward a paved path that led through a grassy field to a grove of trees. As she ambled through the mist, Stacey thought of Helen taking her last walk. What had she been thinking? Why here? It was so peaceful with the only sounds coming from wind whistling in the trees and waves crashing in the distance. Every so often the mist parted and Stacey could see the choppy white caps from the ocean in the distance.

The path turned sharply at the edge of a bluff that overlooked the sea. A gray, weathered, wooden fence provided a safe viewpoint of the swirling water below. Stacey paused. Helen could not have fallen from here by accident. The fence extended along the edge of the bluff as it dipped to a set of wooden steps near the bottom. She would have had to climb over the fence to get to the edge, which was composed of black volcanic rock. It was too sturdy to crumble, but it might be wet and slippery. Heights never disturbed Helen, but she could have slipped. Or had she jumped as authorities told her parents?

Tears flooded Stacey's eyes. What had she expected to find here? Answers? There were none— not any more than what she was discovering at Redfern Manor. Had she let Helen down? If she had made the trip to Evergreen Island when Helen asked, could she have saved her?

"I'm sorry," she whispered to the cliff. Feeling

despondent, Stacey reached into her pocket to get Helen's letter to read it. She searched for a place to sit, not wanting to sit on the fence. She looked back toward her car and stopped. Was that a person along the path? A tall person in a black raincoat? She couldn't tell. Where had they come from? She hadn't heard a car approach.

For a moment terror struck her and then she shook it off. Why should she be afraid?

She looked down trying to decide what to do and finally decided to simply go back to her car. But when she looked up, there was no one there. If someone had been watching her, he or she was gone.

With her breath coming in soft gasps, Stacey hurried back to the parking lot. When she arrived, only her car was parked in the gravel lot. She climbed inside and hit the lock button. Seeing the person had stopped her from reading Helen's letter so she pulled it from her pocket now. Her hands shook though she wasn't certain if it was the cold or the thought that she was holding her friend's last communication in her hand.

Stacey,

I got your message that you aren't able to come. Please try! I should have told you when I visited, but this place is not what I thought, and I can't call and tell you the truth.

The walls here have ears. Peg is a witch who hides it under a sweet veneer. The cook has it out for me and so do her kids, and the handyman keeps following me as though he's afraid I'll find something I shouldn't. Mack terrifies me most of all. He's obsessed with this murder case and I feel I am being dragged into something evil. Like I said in my last letter, I feel Lily Feeney is calling out to me for justice. I never told you but after leaving Portland on my last visit, I went to Los Angeles. I can't write down what I found out but when you come we'll put it all together.

I sense someone here is trying to sabotage my work. Papers disappear, and I'm being watched by more than the handyman. It's like there's a vulture constantly circling me, but he or she stays just below the radar so I can't confront the person. That's why I can't call or email. Don't open those other letters I sent you. Just keep them for now, but bring me that backpack. I really need it.

Come soon. The Kendra crew will solve this thing!

H

"Oh, Helen," Stacey whispered, biting hard on her lip to keep tears from falling. She couldn't imagine what Helen was talking about. Danger? Evil? Someone watching her? But didn't Stacey feel that same paranoia? That spooky figure by the garage or along the foggy path?

She shuddered, peering out the window. There was no one there now. Why would anyone think Helen or she might be a danger? And what could it have to do with Lily Feeney or Redfern Manor? Maybe someone in town or even Del or Mrs. D didn't want the Warrens at the old house. The men at the bar hadn't liked them. Maybe others felt the same. But why go after Helen? Or her for that matter? She re-read the letter, closely studying each line, looking for anything she might have missed, but she couldn't see anything that answered her questions. The second reading only brought more concern.

What other letters was Helen talking about? Stacey hadn't received any mail from her besides this. *Rats!* A new, disturbing thought rattled her. Could her mother have the letters and not realize it? Since moving in with her mother, Stacey had discovered that one of her worst habits was to throw incoming mail into a wooden box and open it once a month.

A sharp rap on her window startled her and Stacey jumped as a face bent down toward her.

Mack!

With shaking fingers, Stacey tossed the letter on the seat, turned on the car and rolled down the window. "What are you doing here?"

"I brought Carlos to the ferry and saw you turn this way. When I didn't see you driving back, I figured maybe you were lost again."

She licked her lips nervously. "I was going for a walk, away from the quarry."

"Do you want me to go with you?"

To her surprise, the thought of walking along the edge of the precipice with Mack beside her bothered her. Was she afraid of him? Not physically. But that strange, physical reaction he sparked in her, well, that was another story. And what if she broke down while thinking of Helen's death?

"Actually, I was just thinking I should get back to the house."

"How's the car working?" he asked, tapping on the open window. "No problems?"

"No, but um…Del said I will have to take it to a mechanic eventually."

"Why don't you do that now? We can leave your car in town and I'll take you home."

She chewed on her lip, considering his proposal. It made sense and she couldn't leave the island until the car was working for certain. "Okay."

****

Once they had taken the car to a nearby shop, Stacey got into Mack's Mercedes for the ride back to Redfern Manor. In the close confines of the car, the silence quickly grew unbearable for Stacey. Mack's large presence seemed to fill up the interior, and she could smell the fresh sea water on his camel hair blazer, as well as the lime scent of his soap. She shivered, despite the fact that heat poured from the car's vents, thinking about using that soap. His soap. There was something intimate about having carried that smell on her own body for hours after bathing in his tub.

"How was your visit with Carlos?" she asked to break the uncomfortable silence. "The two of you seem as close as brothers."

"I suppose he's the closest I'll ever get to having a brother. We worked together for years, but we didn't get to be close friends until after I retired. Now I'm glad he's working in Seattle where he can visit every so often."

She knew how he felt. Helen had been like her sister. "It's important to have a good friend." But it wasn't just thoughts of Helen bothering her. She turned to look out the window. "Were you watching me?"

"What? Why would I be watching you?" His surprise seemed genuine.

"I don't know. I saw someone back...there. Maybe they weren't watching me. It's a public area, so it's no big deal, right? But I did see someone."

"Just like you saw someone outside the garage this morning?"

Irritation pricked at her like a stinging bee. "I'm not imagining these things."

He glanced over at her. "What were you thinking about back there? You seemed a hundred miles away."

She shrugged, looking down at his right hand that rested on the console between them. For a crazy instant she thought about his arm around her the day before when he had pulled her back from the quarry. She shivered again, realizing she was thinking too many personal thoughts about him. He was her boss. She had to keep a professional distance and the easiest way to do that was to insert the subject of their work. "Lily Feeney, of course," she lied. "Do you suppose she walked these paths around here? Think about it. Her family was so well known she probably couldn't go anywhere on the island without someone recognizing her. Maybe that was why she wanted to leave."

He glanced over at her, and she realized he was studying her quickly before turning back to the road. "You're thinking a lot about Lily."

"Isn't that my job?"

His smile was quick and approving. It sent a strange tingle running through her, warming her more than the car's heater. "I think you may be a good fit for this job."

Stacey turned away toward the window, hoping to hide her face from him. She knew it would be a bright red. She resolved to keep her mouth shut for the rest of the trip.

When they reached the house he carried her box inside and placed it beside the stairs. "I'll have Joe take this up to your room. If you're ready, we really should get back to work. We've had enough distractions."

Much as she wanted to go up to her room, Stacey didn't have a chance to protest. Mack was already marching toward the parlor and she followed him. Before she'd left, Stacey had neatly stacked all the folders in one corner so she would know what she had gone through. The neat piles were no longer sitting on the chair. Papers were strewn around the room.

Mack froze. "What the hell?" He turned to her and all his earlier goodwill was gone. "Is this what you call organized?"

Flustered, Stacey stared at the chaos of scattered paper. "Of course not! I...um...you think I did this? No! Someone opened a window or came in here and scattered my work while we were gone."

The incredulous look in Mack's face was like a

slap across the face.

"You don't believe me?"

He waved his left hand at the door. "Are you accusing someone in the house? Because who else could it be?"

Tears formed in her eyes, but Stacey refused to let them fall. The last couple of days he had either been rescuing her or yelling. Was this what Helen had run into?

She drew up and faced him. She might be confused about directions, but she wouldn't be called a liar by anyone.

"I am not a hysterical female who freaks out at the drop of a hat, Mr. Warren. Just because I can't tell right from left, and I almost fell down that quarry... I'm not making things up. I did see a man near the cliff. And...Carlos was in here before he left. He saw how neat it was. Ask him, if you don't believe me."

To her surprise, his look of anger began to dissipate and a smile tugged at his full lips. "I'm sorry, but this seems odd, don't you think? I know you're not hysterical, but it's..."

"What? Strange? Did Helen Stanton ever say she saw or heard anything?"

He drew back, face growing rigid again, and she could see him withdraw. He mumbled something about cleaning up and then lumbered from the room.

Stacey stared at the closed door.

She should not have asked about Helen.

Or maybe he knew someone had been watching her friend?

Maybe he was doing the watching? He seemed to be at the heart of everything.

Originally she ruled out her friend committing suicide because of her personal acquaintance with Helen.

After visiting the site of Helen's death, she was

beginning to rule out an accident. The alternative was ugly, but with all these strange events, a tiny suspicion formed at the back of her head.

Murder?

Chapter Five

Stacey sat on her bed and frowned as she pulled her best black wool skirt from the box of clothes her mother had sent. Given that she had spent the afternoon and evening scooping papers off the floor and putting them into dusty folders, she'd have been better off asking for fresh jeans. At least Mom included plenty of fresh underwear and pajamas.

Oh, no! She cried out in sudden laughter. Her mother had also sent the silk rose nightie Helen had once bought as a gag gift. "Just in case," Helen teased. *In case of what?* Stacey had never been tempted to wear it, not even for Phil.

She grimaced as she thought of Phil. They had been together for five years, even talked about marriage off and on, but he'd never invoked in her the strange tingling sensations she'd been feeling since meeting Mack Warren. She stroked the soft silk, enjoying the smooth touch on her fingers. What would he think of such a gown? A giggle escaped her. *Stupid!* He'd seen her without anything, and as she recalled, what he'd thought had been obvious. He'd been horrified.

But her crazy thoughts about Mack shot quickly from her mind. A corner of an envelope appeared under the matching sheer negligee and she glimpsed Helen's writing. Pushing aside the gown, she yanked out a pile of envelopes, all addressed to her and unopened. A sticky note in her mother's handwriting was stuck to the top envelope.

"Found these in my mail."

No apology, no other comment. With a heavy

sigh of relief, Stacey flipped through them. They were dated shortly after Helen's final visit to Portland. Some were postmarked from Los Angeles. The letters! She found the oldest one and ripped it open. Inside she found a smaller sealed envelope and a one page letter.

Stace,

Please keep the letters I am sending in sealed envelopes. Don't read them. Think of this as our secret adventure—like a Kendra story. I've uncovered some information that I need to keep somewhere safe. I don't trust anyone so I'm sending the notes to you. Don't open them unless I tell you. H

Stacey started to open the sealed envelope, but a quick rap on the door stopped her.

"Stacey?"

At the sound of Mack's voice, she folded the letter and stashed it inside a desk drawer before answering. "Yes?"

"May I come in?"

"Certainly." Too late she noticed the other letters on the bed and made a mad dash to grab them.

Unfortunately he was already entering. His blue eyes narrowed at her quick movements. "Something you would rather I didn't see?"

Her face burned. "No, I just..." Her gaze fell on her sketch pad on the desk and she touched it.

He saw the pad and a quizzical expression crossed his face. "You sketch?"

Wrinkling her nose, she attempted an apologetic shrug. "I try."

"May I look?"

She flipped the sketchbook open and held up the top picture, fearing he might flip back through the book and see the sketch she had drawn of him or worse—Helen.

He studied the picture she had drawn of the

woods after her walk, a charcoal drawing that made them appear dense and forbidding. "I've never thought of our woods that way. This is interesting," he said, stepping back.

Keeping a tight grip on the sketchbook, she thumbed through the pages to a Kendra drawing. "This is my cartoon character I invented. Kind of a super heroine. I call her Kendra."

He nodded as he considered the fanciful drawing. "You have a great imagination. I'm no judge, but you're quite good. You should show this to Peg. She's an artist."

His words of approval sparked a sudden flood of warmth through her limbs. She closed the book and turned away. "I guess I'm embarrassed by my work. My mother calls it doodling." She put the book back on the desk.

His sudden chuckle sent another rush of heat through her. "No. What I do is doodling. That's actual drawing. Anyway, I saw your light on and I wanted to say thank you for taking time to straighten up tonight. Did you get dinner?"

"Mrs. D brought me a sandwich. I didn't mind. I didn't want to fall behind. I told you I am not afraid of hard work."

He turned to leave. "Of course. Don't worry about it." He stopped and drew a deep breath and she followed the direction of his eyes. He was looking at her pile of clothes, more specifically, her filmy rose gown.

To her surprise his face turned as pink as the gown and he moved toward the door as though he could hardly wait to get away from her. "Good night, Stacey."

****

Stacey woke early the next day. She wanted to get away from the house to read the other letters from Helen. She'd thought about them all night but resisted the urge to read them. She kept recalling Helen's letter saying the walls had eyes and ears. What if someone was watching her? Could the room be bugged? She examined the intricate flower buds on the lemon wall paper, wondering if there was a camera lens hidden somewhere. Why had Mack turned up just as she was starting to read the letters?

In surreptitious motions, she stuffed the envelopes into a jacket pocket and headed out as soon as the day turned light. Mrs. D had not arrived so the kitchen was silent. As she stepped onto the porch, the blackened area that outlined the former coach house caught her eye. The trees at the edge of the dark spot were where she had seen someone the previous morning and she walked in that direction. Once she left the pavement the ground was soft and mushy. A fine mist cloaked her. She glanced back toward the house. The windows remained dark. Looking back, she noticed her footprints. Of course! Why hadn't she thought of that before? The person she'd seen would have left footprints in the muddy earth. It could prove she was not imagining things.

The mist was turning to a soft rain and by the time she reached the area, big drops pelted the top of her uncovered head. She drew up the hood of her jacket and walked to where she had seen the person. There were light outlines of large footprints, but the rain was dissolving them.

Rats! Now what? She couldn't get far from the house before she was soaked and the letters in her pocket might get soaked as well. With a reluctant sigh, she turned and started back toward the house just as the Delaney car pulled into the driveway. Joe and Kenny piled out.

Mrs. D's glare was visible even from a distance and Joe waved as she approached. "You nuts?" he said. "It's pouring."

Only Kenny came dashing through puddles to meet her. "Were you looking for stuff?"

"Stuff?"

"From the fire? I found some beads. They wouldn't let me keep 'em and they don't let me go over there. The dead girl burned that place down."

She grimaced. Hearing people accuse Helen of setting fire to the coach house bothered her and it was worse coming from the child.

"Mr. Mack said she was descruntled," he continued.

"Disgruntled," she corrected, "but I don't think she did it."

"How do you know?"

"I heard it was an electrical fire," she replied, recalling Hap's comments.

"Yeah, well, she coulda figured out a way to make it look like that," Joe said. He was unloading grocery bags from the car's trunk and handed one to Kenny.

Stacey reached inside the trunk and looped her hands through the handles of several bags. Joe took the rest and the three made their way up the steps as Mrs. Delaney came out of the kitchen. She reached for the bags from Stacey.

"That's not your job," she said, frowning at Joe.

He lifted a lean shoulder. "She volunteered."

"I don't mind," Stacey said. "I need the exercise."

"You're not like that other girl," Joe said, eyeing her with suspicion. "She screamed if I asked her to carry bread from one room to the next."

"The girls are hired to help Mr. Mack, not do your chores," his mother scolded.

He tossed his bags on the counter, before shuffling back toward the door. The rich scent of coffee filled the room.

"Smells good," Stacey said. "I swear, Mrs. D, everything you cook always smells and tastes so good. I'm worried about gaining weight."

A fleeting smile crossed the woman's face, but she didn't respond. She motioned toward a coffee maker on the counter. "If you get up early and need coffee, just turn it on. I always set it up the night before. I grind the beans in the afternoon before I leave so it's always fresh. Better take off that jacket. You're all wet."

As Stacey started to remove it, she felt the bulge of letters. She buttoned the pocket shut as she hung it on a peg by the door.

Mrs. D poured a cup of coffee and put it on the table in the breakfast nook. "Do you want something now or do you want to wait for the others?"

"I'll wait. Do you need some help? I'm no cook, but I once did prep work at a café." She didn't add it was closed by the health department.

The woman looked surprised at her offer. "No, it's what they pay me for."

Stacey retreated to the table. The coffee mug warmed her cold hands. "How did you come to work for the Warrens?"

"Del and I were working here when the place was a bed and breakfast. It's kinda funny that Mr. Mack is writing that book on Lily. My older sister ran around with her and my mama once worked for old Mrs. Feeney."

"Has he talked to you about Lily?"

"I don't know much. I was pretty young when she left."

A sudden thought hit Stacey. "Did that other researcher ask you about her?"

"All the time. She talked to my sister because Deena was going to Hollywood with Lily. They had a falling out and Deena got married instead."

"Deena never saw Lily after she left?"

"Sure. Deena and Ray went to California for a visit, but it didn't go well. They broke up when they got back and I think it had something to do with Lily."

"Did you tell this to Mack?"

"Helen asked the same thing." She laughed suddenly, a harsh sound, more like a bark. "Like maybe it coulda had something to do with her death."

"Helen's?"

The woman looked at her, face quizzical. "What the hell are you talking about?"

Stacey realized her mistake at once. "I'm sorry if I'm confusing you. I meant Lily's."

The woman's face hardened. "I'm sure it didn't and I don't appreciate strangers spreading gossip. I don't even know why I told you about that. It's none of your business. Deena's happily married. Got two good kids and a good man. She's lucky she didn't go with Lily or stay with Ray."

"What happened to Ray?" The name had gone right by her the first time Mrs. D said it, but now Stacey remembered the men at the Gull's Roost mentioning Ray. Helen had been looking for him.

Mrs. D. grunted. "That stupid fool went back to Hollywood after Lily and ended up in jail. Now I ain't gonna talk about it anymore."

Stacey finished her coffee in silence and headed back toward her room. As she passed the parlor door, she stopped. Maybe she should check to make certain her work from the previous night had not been disturbed again. She peered inside and smiled. The boxes rested untouched on the floor. One good thing had come from the mess. As she put the papers back into their proper folders she'd checked for Feeney notes. She'd found nothing, but now she was finished with those boxes.

She continued toward her room, pausing at the top of the stairs. All the doors were closed, but as she looked toward Mack's room, a flash of light caught her eye. It came from under the door to her right—the door to the third floor. Was someone up there? The light flashed again. She stepped to the door and turned the knob. As Mack said, the door was locked. She leaned close to the door, listening, but the light went off, as though it had been extinguished.

A click sounded down the hall and she whirled around as Peg's door opened.

"You're up early," Peg said.

"I went for a walk."

"That's crazy. It's pouring rain."

"I know. My jacket got soaked..." She clapped her hand to her mouth. She'd left the letters in the jacket pocket! Given Helen's warnings and the weird things that kept happening, she needed to get them.

"What's wrong?" Peg asked, as though sensing Stacey's discomfort.

"I forgot something." She hopped down the stairs ahead of Peg. Not wanting to remove the letters in front of an audience, she grabbed her damp coat from the hook and whirled around. By now Peg had reached the kitchen.

She crossed to the coffee machine, but she was watching Stacey. "You forgot your jacket? I don't think you'll need it upstairs."

"Did you find something when you were poking around at the coach house?" Mrs. D asked.

"No."

Peg stopped pouring coffee and focused her attention on Stacey. "What? You were at the coach house?"

Stacey grimaced, silently cursing the older woman. Or maybe she was getting even with her for being so nosy about Ray and Deena. "I was looking around. Mack said Helen Stanton put things on a flash drive. They're so small..."

Peg's voice was sharp as she began to stir sugar into her coffee. "Del and Mack conducted a thorough search for that flash drive. You don't need to waste time on that."

"She's the curious sort," Mrs. Delaney said from the stove where she was cracking eggs into a bowl. "She asked me about Lily."

"Really?"

"For the book, you know," Stacey said.

Peg's face grew into a rigid mask and she dropped the spoon on the counter with a clatter. "I hired you to organize, keep notes and transcribe. I didn't hire you to investigate."

"I know, but—"

"No arguments. If you start playing games, I'll let you go. Simple as that." Her teeth clenched together. "Do you understand?"

Stacey couldn't answer. She nodded and hugging her coat to her, she rushed toward the door.

****

She was still reeling from Peg's display of temper as she stood in the hot shower letting the stinging spray warm her up. How stupid of her to be so open. Had Helen done the same thing? Could her curiosity have led to her death? Could the answer to Helen's death be in those letters? She needed to read them, but how?

When she came out of the shower wrapped in her robe, Stacey made a decision. She locked her bedroom door and slid the letters from her jacket. She took them into the bathroom and locked that door too. Certainly they wouldn't put a camera in the bathroom, would they?

She re-opened the first letter and this time she unsealed the inner envelope. It was a single typed page, dated a month before Helen's last visit.

Lily Feeney's body
Throat slashed — like others
Posed in sexual position — like others
Piece of hair cut — like others

Left ring finger sliced off — different than others
Killed after midnight — not like others
Not as much blood — killed elsewhere?
Witnesses heard screams
Dark-haired man and dark sedan
Composite drawing?

Stacey frowned. Was this what Helen had been doing? Or were these comments she had copied from John Scotti's notes? Stacey looked at the other letters. Mack said she was taking notes and compiling an overall file. Could this be the information?

Wait until she told him! But how could she admit Helen had sent this to her? No, wait. A better plan would be to pretend to locate the notes in the boxes downstairs. That would show him Helen had not been lying. Stacey hesitated. She didn't want to give him the letters until she'd had a chance to read the information. Helen had sent it to her for safe keeping instead of giving it to him for a reason. She needed to figure out why.

She opened the next letter.

Hang onto this and put it with the others I send you. H

This was a typed transcript of an interview that Helen had conducted in Los Angeles. The man was a bartender at a place called the Pink Chariot and described Lily as a regular customer, *"a party girl always looking for fun."* The next transcription was an interview with Lily's landlady. It was interspersed with italicized notes from Helen. Apparently the woman wanted to protect her tenants, but she had told Helen about Lily having various male visitors.

"A different man every night. Sometimes she threw wild parties. Not surprised at what happened to her." What would Mack think of those comments?

There appeared to be several relationships but

none lasted long. Only one got special attention. *"Boyfriend #5, terrible fights. Broke up one month before she died. He was in show biz. Promised to help her get a job, and threatened once to throw her out the window. Police called, but no charges were filed. "*

Stacey sighed. Did Mack know any of this?

A sudden pounding on the bedroom door made her jump. She folded up the letter and opened the bathroom door. "Yes?"

"Are you going to work today or spend it locked in your room pouting?" Mack called from outside the bedroom.

"I'll be right down," she called. Guilt sliced through her. *Rats!* She'd lost track of time and it was after nine. She donned black slacks, a black-and-brown striped cardigan sweater and hurried to the parlor. Mack was pacing the floor. He looked up, his face a dull shade of crimson. It made the scar along his right cheek stand out in a thin, white line.

"I thought I made myself clear about being prompt."

"I'm sorry," she said, brushing her hand through her limp hair, which she hadn't had a chance to dry or style. "I got up early and fell asleep after showering."

"Ghosts keeping you up?" he asked, but there was no hint of humor.

She tried a smile but it died under the face of his cold stare. "Maybe."

He didn't react. "Let's work on those boxes over there." He pointed to a line of sagging boxes under the window. "I think Helen had started working on them. I'm going back upstairs."

"Did Peg…"

"Yes." He sighed, running his hand through his hair. "I'm going to make a quick apology for my sister, because she's acting on my orders. I need someone to type and organize, not ask questions or make judgments. I thought I'd made that clear the last few days."

Stacey felt deflated as he walked out the door. No wonder Helen had grown discouraged. He was treating her as though she was some sort of robot. She was tempted to tear up the notes Helen had written. Instead, as she sorted through the first box, she removed Helen's pages she'd hidden in the pocket of her sweater and slid them into the file.

Drawing a deep breath she crossed to the intercom and pressed the talk button. "Mack? I found some notes."

"What?" He sounded irritated.

"I think I found Helen's notes about Lily."

"I'll be right down."

Mack's handsome face was expectant as he entered the room. She explained where she'd found them and waited as he read the pages.

A smile crossed his face. In fact he began to beam. He turned to Stacey and caught her up in a spontaneous hug. Just as quickly he moved away from her, but his smile didn't diminish.

"Good going! You're exactly right. Did you see anything like that in the papers you sorted yesterday?"

"No. But there may be more in this box. I noticed they were crammed in there, like she was trying to stuff them somewhere. Maybe she was hiding them?"

His face stiffened into a stern mask of displeasure. "Hiding them from whom?"

"I don't know. Someone who was trying to keep her from finding the truth?"

He grew very still, the papers gripped in his left hand. When he spoke his voice was very soft, but hard as steel. "Find out what truth?"

"About Lily, about her death. That's an interview with a bartender about Lily."

He lifted his right hand to his temple as though she was giving him a head ache and gestured for her to sit down at her desk. He pulled over the visitor chair to sit beside her. "There are a few things I need to tell you about Helen Stanton."

Her breath caught. What should she do if he answered all her questions? Quit and go home? But as she looked at the sadness in his blue eyes that only came to light when he was talking about Lily Feeney, she realized she couldn't. He looked forlorn, like a lost boy. Would he be content forever to sit in this house writing books about dead people like Lily Feeney or the police detective, John Scotti? What about starting a new life for himself? She didn't have much of one herself, but she couldn't imagine leaving him buried here with no one but his grumpy sister and Mrs. D for company and infrequent visits from Carlos.

"What about her?" she asked.

He flipped through the pages and tapped them against his knee. "This is good work, but it's not what she was hired to do. I know you probably think I'm an ogre for giving you rules and re-emphasizing things, but there's a reason for it."

"Because of Helen? Didn't you like her?"

His face burst into a smile, and she was pleased to see that. "I enjoyed her enthusiasm when she started. She was excited about the project. I think she figured I could get her a job in television after we completed this. She had a degree in communications."

Stacey knew that was why Helen had been excited about the opportunity to work with Mack. She had no reply and he went on as though he didn't expect one.

"Helen got very caught up in my interview with Greenlee and his claim that he didn't kill Lily. As she organized John's notes, she suddenly decided maybe he was telling the truth and then set out to prove that someone else did it. She was convinced she could find the real killer."

Stacey had started to surmise as much from Helen's letters. Was that information in one of those sealed envelopes? "What did she find out?"

He gestured at the cluttered room. "I don't know. I told her, like I told you, that I wanted nothing to leave this room. I discovered she'd removed John's notes to copy them for her own use. But she wasn't hired to solve the damn case. Now the notes are missing."

Stacey couldn't stop her smile. That was all so like Helen. "She was trying to show you she could be an investigative journalist, just like you."

He ignored the comment, his voice growing grim. "She went to Los Angeles without my knowledge to track down people who knew Lily and interview them."

"It sounds like she was resourceful."

"That was a waste of my time and her money," he said through gritted teeth. "I would have done those interviews myself, but in a different manner. I wanted to know about the lighter side of Lily's life. Now these people may not talk to me or give me what I need."

"But they painted an honest picture of Lily."

He gripped the pages in his fist and pounded his leg with them. "This was not what I had in mind."

"Do you think she found something?" Stacey asked. "Is that why you're so upset?"

"What are you saying?" he asked, lips twitching into a sad smile. "That I'm angry because she found something I'd missed? Professional jealousy?"

She touched his arm without thinking. "Maybe you're still that investigative reporter but you don't want to admit it?"

He glanced down at her hand and she pulled it

away with a mumbled apology. He lurched to his feet and walked to the door without looking back. "Keep going through those boxes. Let me know if you find anything else."

Chapter Six

Following the tense morning, Stacey took a quick break after lunch. She needed to read through more of Helen's letters so she put on her jacket and walked outside. Seeing Del in the greenhouse she turned toward the garage. Maybe she could find a spot to be alone.

As she neared the long stone structure she heard shouts and a thud. Fearing someone in trouble, she burst into the side door. To her surprise, this wasn't a part of the garage. It was a large open room with athletic equipment scattered about and one full mirrored wall. Hadn't Del said something about a gym?

Joe stood beside a hanging full length punching bag. He stood back and directed a kick at it, shouting as he did so. As he whirled, he saw her. He kicked the bag again, emitting another shout.

"What do you want?" he asked.

"What are *you* doing?"

"Kick boxing," he explained, launching another kick. "It's the only good thing about coming out here. Del set this up for Mr. Mack, but he never uses it."

She examined the state of the art equipment—two treadmills, two stationary bikes, rows of weights, mats, an elliptical machine and another, smaller punching bag. "Would you teach me how to do that?"

He blinked, looking at her as though she had lost her mind. "Why?"

"Why not? I need the exercise. Is that such a strange request?"

"You don't look the type."

Actually she wasn't, though she liked the idea of working out. Her mother's complex had a gym she used regularly and she needed something to counteract Mrs. D's cooking.

As she watched Joe, the kick boxing appealed to her. Kendra did it in her cartoons. Maybe she needed to learn what went into actually doing it. "I'm going to get permission from Peg to use the gym and get changed, okay?"

He grinned, shaking his shaggy hair. "They don't mind since they don't use the place. There are some clean shorts and t-shirts hanging on the wall, if you want."

Maybe it was better not to tell anyone. Stacey changed in an adjoining washroom and rejoined Joe. She attempted a kick at the bag and nearly lost her footing as she missed. Joe laughed and directed her. This time, her kick landed.

"Ow!" she screeched, tumbling to her knees.

Joe stood over her and smiled. "Not quite what you thought, is it?"

She climbed to her feet, determined to try again. Another successful kick at the bag brought a searing pain to her calf and another cry.

Joe took a deep breath. "Are you ready for me to show you how to do this?"

"Show me."

Slowly he explained how to hit the bag with maximum impact, but less pain for her. He showed her how to properly position her legs and feet. By the time they quit after an hour of work, Stacey felt pummeled and exhausted, but she was smiling as she walked out the door. This was the sort of action Kendra/Helen would take.

As they sat in the kitchen, sipping iced tea, Stacey looked at Joe. "Does your mother ever talk about Lily Feeney?"

"Only to say she was a trouble maker who probably had it coming. I guess she stole Aunt Deena's boyfriend or something."

"Are any of Lily's relatives still around?"

"Nah. They all moved away, but some of her school chums are still around. I think Mr. Mack talked to 'em."

"Do you think Lily or one of the Feeneys haunt Redfern Manor?"

Joe looked up toward the high beamed ceiling. "Nah. All them old Feeneys died happy and rich. Lily wanted outta here so why would she come back? You saying you've seen ghosts?"

Stacey drew a shuddering breath and shrugged. She didn't think Joe would believe her about lights and shadowy images, but then he emitted a strange, guttural laugh.

"Maybe it's Helen Stanton."

Stacey's face whipped toward him. "Why would she haunt Redfern Manor?"

His brown eyes shifted back and forth across the table and when he spoke, he kept his voice just above a whisper. "What if she didn't commit suicide? You know? What if she was murdered?"

Stacey almost dropped her glass onto the table. "Why do you say that?"

He glanced around again, as though afraid of being overheard and gestured with a palm to keep her voice down. "Sometimes I wonder. She ran off toward the quarry after a fight with Mr. Mack. Then later she's found at the bottom of the cliff on the other side of the island? People said she mighta walked there, but it's over five miles. She didn't like walking in the woods. Why would she walk all the way to the other side of the island?"

"Maybe someone drove her," Stacey offered.

"Or maybe she took a ride with the wrong person," he added.

"Joe!"

Peg's sharp voice from the dining room door drew them both up. "That is the silliest thing I've ever heard. Now stop it!" She glared at Stacey. "Shouldn't you be working instead of sitting in here trading idiotic stories?"

****

Stacey returned to the parlor feeling chagrined at Peg's latest outburst of anger. Yet she couldn't shake Joe's comments. He seemed to have his own doubts about Helen's death. She could hardly wait until their next kick boxing lesson. They'd agreed to meet again early the next morning and she intended to question him further.

Would Peg tell Mack what they'd been discussing? He walked into the parlor in the late afternoon, giving no indication that he knew. He handed her several dictation tapes and set up the recorder so she could begin transcribing.

In the middle of the explanation, her phone buzzed.

Mack's head jerked up. "What's that?"

"My cell phone." She frowned at the instrument on her desk. It only worked every so often. Why now when he was around? She looked at the number in caller ID as it buzzed again. Phil. *Rats!* Just what she didn't need with Mack sitting nearby.

"Go ahead and answer it," he said, though his voice was tense.

Phil launched into a tirade the instant she said hello. "This is the craziest thing you've ever done. To take off to Washington and get a job without even talking to us about it."

"I needed work," she began.

"Listen, Stace, your mother and I have decided we're coming to get you. Give us your address and we'll be there tomorrow."

His peremptory tone bothered her, but she

couldn't argue at the moment. She looked over at Mack. His back was stiff. "It's not that simple."

"Of course it is. When you come home we'll resume our wedding plans."

"No, Phil!" Her voice rang out louder than she'd intended and she hopped to her feet. He was the one who had stopped their earlier plans, but she couldn't continue this conversation with Mack listening. She stepped to the door, hoping he'd understand and walked into the hall before resuming the conversation. "I'm fine, okay?"

He didn't answer and she rushed on. "I have a job and a place to stay. I don't need help."

Again there was no answer and she lowered the phone. The screen read "call ended."

When had it hung up? When she walked out the door? It didn't matter. He wouldn't have listened to her. She'd call back and leave a message. She changed the ring tone to silent and stepped back into the parlor to resume her work.

Mack glanced up at her, his face a cool mask. "Something wrong?"

Stacey attempted a smile. "Not really. Mack, can I ask a favor?"

A fleeting shadow crossed his brow. "More time off?"

"Not really. Um...it's about the gym...do you mind if I use it?"

He blinked rapidly, looking toward the door.

She tried to smile though her face felt stiff. "See...I'm going to gain weight if Mrs. D keeps feeding me, so I need to work out. Why did you have it built?"

He looked down at his folded right hand. "Physical therapy, they told me."

She squeezed her eyes shut. How stupid. She should have guessed that. "Well, maybe we should build a workout schedule into our day?" The words rushed out. "Physical ther...exertion might be just the thing to help us both clear our heads."

He stared at her for a minute and then slowly a smile slid across his lips. "You may be right. Let's start first thing tomorrow."

****

Stacey realized the next morning that with Mack's presence she couldn't question Joe, but it did improve the tension in their working relationship. He seemed to enjoy watching her kickboxing efforts and she was surprised to see he did have more mobility in his right side than she realized.

There was one problem. After the second day he had been working out so hard, he was sweating profusely. He yanked off his t-shirt and fanned himself with his hand. She found herself staring at his hard chest, coated in a thin cover of sandy blond hair. He must have worked out fairly regularly because his stomach was flat and the muscles of his wide shoulders were muscular and thick. Her breath caught and he jerked his head up and their gaze met. She turned away quickly, her face growing warm.

"Sorry," he said. "It's not a pretty sight, is it?"

She blinked and glanced back as he covered his right side with his t-shirt. "No, it's..." she stopped. She had been so focused on the strength and view of his bare body she had not really noticed the criss-cross of scars that ran down his right side. "It's not the scars; I mean the accident must have been awful, but..." She was rambling, she knew, so she just slammed her mouth shut. Her reaction had been to his overall body, not the scars, but how could she explain that without looking like a worse fool?

"That's enough for today," he said in a crisp tone. "Let's get back to work."

****

The days began to fall into a predictable pattern.

Fearing her mother might show up, Stacey left a message on both her mother's and Phil's voice mail that she was moving to a new job in Seattle and would call them when she got settled. Not that she could leave. Her car remained in the shop so she was confined to Redfern Manor. The house continued to make her uneasy. A couple of times she heard noises on the third floor, but saw no more strange lights or strangers outside by the burned carriage house area. Every time she turned the handle on the door to the stairs, it was locked.

She went through several more letters from Helen but they didn't reveal any critical information. The interviews were with people who knew Lily from the Purple Chariot. The women weren't close to her and two accused her of trying to steal their boyfriends. All of the men claimed they'd slept with her. Stacey didn't like the picture she got of Lily from the letters, but it made her more of a possible Greenlee victim. If she was into casual sex, perhaps she'd hooked up with him just like the other women he'd killed.

Stacey placed the letters into various files and pretended to find them for Mack. Most of her days were spent sorting through the boxes and typing up dictation and transcripts of Mack's interviews. She loved listening to the soft rich tones of his voice, but the interviews were boring. He'd talked to Lily's teachers and friends, but they made Lily seem so bland. Why was he so fascinated with this colorless character? Even his Hollywood interviews with her old director and several cast mates didn't shed as much light on her as Helen's interviews.

Her own attempts to find out about Lily ended in disaster—like her discussion with Del. She'd gone to the greenhouse hoping to read more of Helen's letters. He came in as she finished.

"You lookin' for me?" he asked.

She had no reason to be there so she fingered a nearby tulip. "I was just admiring the flowers."

"Sure. I figured you wanted me to drive you somewhere since you don't have your car. That Helen was always goin' somewhere. If she didn't have gas she'd hitch a ride or make me take her. But I ain't no chauffeur."

"I'm not like Helen," she said, feeling disloyal to her friend. "I was just thinking you do a great job with these flowers. The house always smells so good."

"You trying to butter me up?" he asked, giving her a skeptical glance. "Like Helen?"

"Did she ask you about Lily?"

"Why should she? I didn't know Lily."

"What about Ray?"

He turned to her, his face darkening, eyes narrowed. "What the hell business of that is yours?"

"I understand you're Ray's cousin, and he knew her."

"It ain't no one's business. Lily ruined Ray. If that guy hadn't killed her..." He stopped as though realizing he'd said too much.

"Did you tell that to Helen?"

Del threw up his hands in anger. "You get out of here. I got no time for you. And don't be telling Mr. Mack I was rude either. Helen threatened to get me fired, but she learned that ain't gonna happen. You do your job and let me do mine. And leave Ray alone. What happened between him and Lily was years ago. You mess with him, you'll learn a lesson you don't wanna learn!"

The confrontation left her shaking. Had Helen found Ray and angered him? Could he have had something to do with Lily's death? Was he the angry boyfriend mentioned in the landlady's comments? Stacey wanted to see Helen's notes again but she couldn't ask for them. She was beginning to understand what Helen had been up against. What had she discovered and could it have played a role in her death?

****

Mack's frown as he examined the pages she had just finished typing soured Stacey's already fluttering stomach. What could be wrong with them? She'd worked so hard on that dictation and run it through spell check.

"Is...something wrong?" she finally asked. "Did I miss something?"

He shook his head. "No. I was quoting from some of John's notes and this doesn't make sense." He took out a pen and circled something on the pages. "There's a problem with the time. Greenlee met all his victims shortly after he got off work at nine. According to this, Lily's landlady put her at home that night until one. It means Lily couldn't have met Greenlee the night she was killed. Maybe Helen got the time wrong. That's what I get for trusting an amateur. I'll have to call the woman back."

Blaming Helen again. But at least whatever was disturbing him was not Stacey's fault. Some of the sourness dissolved. "I could do that."

"No," he replied, voice firm. "I'll do it. I'm not taking any more chances." He picked up another stack of papers.

Stacey went back to her work, but her nerves felt on edge and the pages blurred before her eyes.

"Good!" he said suddenly and her head jerked up.

"What?"

"You got quite a bit done. I didn't expect you to finish transcribing all that dictation. You are fast."

Stacey's breath caught as she stared at him. They'd been working so close together for the past few days and the surge of warmth that rushed through her surprised her. What kept happening to her? His approval and the smile that creased his full lips often sent a strange spark of awareness through her that left her feeling weightless. And it was happening more and more every day. "Thank you."

He gave the page another quick glance and winked at her. "You know, I might actually want to keep your around."

The strange spark smoldering inside her erupted into a full-fledged brush fire. She stared at his face, at the warmth that glowed in his blue eyes. His lips were turned up in a full grin and she could see his white teeth through his slightly parted pink full lips. For a crazy instant she wondered what it would be like to have those lips touch hers. Would they be warm, enticing? Oh, rats, they already were.

Her breath caught and she jerked her head down. His sudden chuckle that rumbled through him only made her feel warmer, like a simmering fire was developing inside her, smoldering and growing. *Oh, rats, oh rats, oh rats!*

****

That morning was just the beginning of a frightening new awareness of Mack. Not that she'd been immune to him before but she was getting into new territory for her. She'd never been so aware of a man. In some ways, these crazy sensations that erupted every time she was around Mack made her think her relationship with Phil had been downright cold. She was no blushing virgin, but her nights with Phil had never made her feel as warm as one glance from Mack could. Every time she looked at Mack's large hands, she wondered what it would be like to be touched by him and it made her insides grow liquid at times. Phil had never done that.

The next evening she found Mack sitting in front of a blazing fire in the drawing room. He stared into the flames, arms crossed, body stiff. She hesitated, but he turned and saw her in the doorway. A flicker of surprise crossed his stern features.

"Stacey, I didn't hear you come in."

"I'm sorry. I...uh, just wanted to get a book," she said, gesturing at the book case along the back wall. She had heard Peg upstairs and thought he'd gone over to the mainland so she'd have the lower area to herself for once. She hadn't heard him return.

He waved at the empty wing chair across from him. "Please don't let me chase you away. Sitting in front of the fire can be quite soothing." He didn't look that relaxed. He wore a light blue dress shirt and loosened burgundy tie and the wool slacks from a charcoal suit.

She sank onto the chair, uncertain what to say. She chewed on her lower lip to keep from blurting something stupid.

Mack leaned back in the chair and a smile slid across his lips. In the glow of the fire, a soft glow seemed to come into his eyes. "It gets lonely living here with just my sister for company. I always realize that when I go off the island. Tell me about yourself."

She shrugged. "There's not much to say..."

"Nonsense. Tell me about your drawing. How long have you been an artist?"

To her surprise there seemed an honest interest in his eyes, which had gone to a soft blue shade, sort of like an inviting lake in the summer time in the Cascade Mountains.

"Oh, as long as I can recall."

"And Kendra?"

Stacey smiled at his recollection of her heroine. "She grew up with me. She's always had fabulous adventures." A rush of heat crossed her face. Hopefully the light was low enough in the room that he couldn't see the red color invading her face. This morning she'd drawn Kendra with a new man in her life. A tall, fierce blond warrior with bright eyes and full lips and a charming grin. Kendra was falling in love!

His chuckle made her cheeks grow warmer. "I like that idea. What about you? Do you have adventures?"

"Oh, no! I'm just...me. Dull, boring."

He shook his head. "No. Something tells me you're far from boring. Something tells me there's more hiding behind your Kendra drawings."

She shook her head. "I don't understand."

"Come on, Stacey, don't we all have something we try to hide? What is your secret?"

The fire crackled, and she jumped. "I don't know what you mean."

"Uh-huh," he said with a mocking laugh.

She turned to him. "What about you? What are your secrets?"

He turned back to the fire and his jaw tightened. The scar along the side of his face cast a shadow along the lower right side, and the scar beside his upper brow seemed to grow as his forehead wrinkled into a frown. "You don't want to know my secrets. They're too dark."

She looked down at her hands, unable to face him. "It must be tough to lose someone close to you."

"Damn tough. It rips at your insides. Until your heart feels like it's about to be ripped out by powerful hands. Hopefully you'll never lose someone..."

"I...lost a friend..." The words seemed to tumble from her mouth before she could stop them. "One minute she was there and...then she was gone."

"An accident?"

She nodded, her breath coming a little faster.

"So you know about regrets. Things you wish you'd said. Things you wish you hadn't."

She looked up at Mack and in that moment she knew he wasn't the hard man she'd been fearing since she arrived. This was a man with deep feelings who had been hurt when he lost his wife and child. No wonder he still wore his wedding band. Her heart lurched.

He reached over and touched the top of her hand. "I'm sorry. I'm being morbid."

"No, I think of her all the time. She was like Kendra. Alive, exciting…"

"Is she your model for Kendra?"

"Yes."

He studied her until she grew uncomfortable and looked away, focusing on the leaping flames in the fireplace.

"Enough feeling morose. We need to compose an adventure where Kendra becomes a goddess of goodness, sort of like you."

"Me?" A pleasant streak of surprise raced through her.

"Bright and sunny," he said with a crooked smile.

Stacey's face remained warm, but now her insides were catching fire too. "Is that how you see me?"

"Aren't you?"

It was how she wanted to be, but that was more how she saw Helen.

"I'm going to assign Kenny to work with you tomorrow," he added. "To help you with your adventure. He has lots of great ideas and he likes you. That's how you can always tell a good person. Kids are great judges."

Her gaze slid around the dimly lit room with its austere antiques and dark furniture. "What about you? How can we brighten up your life?"

Again, the frown transformed him into a brooding gothic hero from a Kendra adventure. "I'm sorry, young Stacey. I don't think that's possible."

Stacey leaned toward him, wishing she could share some of the warmth he engendered within her with him. "Yes, it is. You say everyone is hiding some dark secret, well, I say everyone has something bright inside them. A little ray of sunshine they may be hiding. They just need help bringing it out. Maybe that's what you need. Kenny likes you too."

His gaze met hers and moved over her face, but in those brief seconds she could see it softening. Her heart did a wild flip flop as though it was a giant pancake inside her chest. The fingers of his left hand reached out and a gentle finger tip stroked the edge of her cheek and traced a slow line to her lips. The thudding in her chest became a wild thumping of her heart and her breath caught in an audible gasp.

The corners of his lips quirked into a smile and Mack leaned toward her. For a crazy second she thought he might be going to kiss her, but he suddenly took a deep breath and dropped his hand. He jerked to his feet, moving away, his limp pronounced. "Sorry, Stacey, I don't think I'll ever find anything bright enough to light the darkness inside me."

Feeling as though she was in a trance, Stacey rose and caught his right arm. "Mack, wait."

It was a breathless plea and she feared he might pull away from her. Instead, he looked down at her and their gaze held for a crazy, heart stopping minute. As she stared at him, she felt like she wanted to lift that shadow over his heart. To make him see the good things, to stop him from spending his time with a ghost. Was that dark shadow why he was so focused on Lily Feeney?

"Mack...I would like..." she said with a strangled voice, unable to vocalize what she wanted to say.

He put his fingers on her hand, and she feared

he meant to remove it but instead he pressed them against her skin and then lifted his hand to take hold of her face again.

This time when he started to lean toward her she didn't wait. Stacey pressed toward him, lifting her mouth to his. The touch of his lips was soft against hers and with a groan in his chest, his arm came around her pulling her to him.

She wrapped her arms around his neck, opening her lips to his, letting his moist tongue slide inside her mouth. She felt tingly all over like she was about to become a five foot column of hot liquid flowing down onto the floor. Her moan surprised her and she almost giggled, but instead she pushed against him, feeling the strength in his hard body against her.

A sudden thump on the floor above them stopped them both.

He drew back as though someone had stepped between them and Stacey almost slid to the floor. He caught her arms in his, righting her...

"Ghosts?" he asked with a sly smile.

"Maybe... but this time you heard it too at least."

He nodded and pulled back further. "I'm sorry. That was out of line. We can't do this, not if we have to work together." He turned and moved away from her to the edge of the fire place. "Good night, Stacey."

She wanted to go to him, to say she didn't care if he was her boss. But the fire inside her burned so fiercely she feared saying or doing something totally stupid—like yanking off her clothes and begging him to make love to her right there on the floor in front of the fire.

She'd never been so forward with a man as she had been when she pressed herself to him.

With fears of unleashing her crazy thoughts, she dropped her head and hurried to the door in quick steps.

As she hopped up the steps with her insides still flaming, she could almost hear Helen laughing.

"Stacey, you nut, you're falling in love with Mack Warren."

Chapter Seven

Thump!

The sudden sound jerked Stacey out of a sound sleep. She sat up in bed and looked at the ceiling of her room. Her heart was already pounding from the startling noise but a sudden scraping above her like the scraping of a chair made it pound harder. What in the world?

"Mack?" she called, but there was only silence and the scraping stopped. She pulled the sheet up over her arms, feeling a sudden chill. Looking down, she made a face. She wore the rose colored silk gown and she felt silly all of a sudden. Imagine if Mack was to answer her or even to knock at her door at that minute! What would she tell him? She'd been so overcome by his kiss the night before she'd gone to bed with crazy, romantic thoughts in her head? Inappropriate thoughts, she decided now in the light of day.

Quickly she rose from her bed, keeping an eye on the ceiling. Was someone up there? Maybe she needed to check. She pulled on her robe and tiptoed to the door. She yanked it open just as Mack opened his door and stepped into the hall. He wore a forest green turtleneck over dark slacks and his blond hair was neatly combed. She sucked in a breath at how together he could look so early in the morning. He looked down the hall at her and cleared his throat.

"Good morning," he said in a crisp tone, lowering his gaze immediately. "I'm going downstairs to get coffee, but I'll be working up here the rest of the day."

Was that because he felt as silly as she did over their close moments the previous night? Heck, she was still having them, drinking in his appearance like warm morning cocoa.

As he drew closer and she didn't reply, his brow furrowed. "Something wrong?"

Licking her lips, as her throat became parched, she pointed at the ceiling. "I thought I heard something up there."

He looked up and then rolled his eyes and shook his head. "You're dreaming," he said curtly. He drew closer, studying her and then stopped and turned away, color rising in his cheeks. She looked down and realized her robe had fallen open and he could see the flimsy rose gown.

She pulled her robe tighter around her and decided this wasn't the time to argue with him. "I heard this noise above me. It woke me…"

He shook his head and she wasn't going to argue. She stepped back inside her door and closed it quickly. How stupid of her!

A floorboard creaked above her, but she wouldn't open the door again. Maybe he was right. Maybe she was dreaming. Certainly she had gone to sleep with thoughts of his sudden kiss. And she was still infected with whatever passionate fever grabbed her the previous evening.

"Stupid," she whispered as she headed for the bathroom to take a shower, pulling off the flimsy gown. Sleeping in it wouldn't make him come to her or even want her. He'd seemed totally uninterested a minute ago, uncomfortable even. She'd better get over these fervent feelings. Helen had never told her he was particularly sexy, but after those moments the previous night, she certainly felt that way. Would her blood temperature ever grow cool being around him? It had to, and it better happen soon! She turned the water to cold as she stepped under the spray.

****

True to his word, Mack sent Kenny to look at her Kendra drawings that morning as she took her mid-morning break. She retrieved them from her room and took them down to the parlor to let him go through the latest batch.

"Cool," the chubby, towheaded boy said, flipping pages in her sketchbook. "Hey, this looks like Helen."

Why hadn't she remembered that was there? "Helen?"

"Yeah, the girl who died."

She attempted to laugh, though it sounded false. "That's created from my imagination."

He turned to another page and she relaxed. It was a recent picture she'd drawn of Kendra and her new warrior in battle.

"I like this," Ken said with an approving grin. "But you need to make that guy more fierce."

Hoping to distract him from his discovery of Helen, she picked up the tablet. He was right. And she needed to make him look less like Mack. Sooner or later with his quick eye that had picked out Helen he would see the resemblance to her boss.

"Let's work on the villain," she said. "What shall we name him?"

"How about Lord Verdone?" Kenny offered.

"Where did you get that?"

"My imagination."

She laughed at his intensity. "Sounds good. Want to help with the princess who needs to be saved?" She began sketching in new figures, staying away from any resemblance to Helen or Mack. By the time they shared their project with Mack later that afternoon, she and Kenny had composed a battle that was unlike anything she had ever drawn. When Mack smiled in approval, Stacey felt like the sun had burst through a fogbank.

****

For the next few days Stacey spent more time with the little boy than with Mack. He spent most of the days and even his nights locked in his room, having Mrs. D take up his dinner. He told her over the intercom he was on a writing roll and didn't want to stop, but she feared it was more that he wanted to put distance between them.

The absence only fueled Stacey's thoughts about him, but she forced herself to focus on doing a good job on her filing, working harder with Joe in the gym and more with Kenny on her drawings.

Even though her senses all seemed to come alive whenever she was around Mack, he had returned to being cool and impersonal, as though reminding her they were together only for their work. None of his comments were personal or even teasing and she forced herself to act as business-like as possible. The only time she saw him even crack a smile was when she and Kenny shared their work with him.

But her growing success with Kenny was more than offset by sudden problems with Peg. Suddenly she found fault with everything Stacey did. She complained that Stacey tracked in mud, even though Joe was the culprit. Stacey kept his secret and she also didn't tell Peg he was the one who devoured the strawberries Peg cleaned to make strawberry shortcake.

But it was the pot roast that made Peg most angry.

Stacey had carried her cup of coffee to the table and slipped into a chair in the breakfast nook as she did most mornings. Of all rooms in the old house, except for the turret which she couldn't visit, she liked the kitchen best. Maybe it was because of the tall French windows that let in the morning sun when it was visible or the nook in front of the windows with its white wooden table and chairs with comfortable, green cushions. The kitchen walls were exposed brick and tall white cabinets lined two of the walls. A center island provided cooking and preparation space. A set of stairs occupied one corner, but no one used them. Joe informed her they led directly to another locked door on the third floor.

Mrs. Delaney stood at the stove, putting eggs into a skillet.

"Do you ever wonder if the house is haunted?" Stacey asked.

The woman jerked around and frowned at her. "What?"

"Do you ever think there might be a ghost...you know, one of the Feeneys?"

Her cackling laugh was quick, unusual for the older woman. "Dear, you've been reading the pamphlets. They hinted at ghosts to make visitors feel like there was something special about this old house. In all the years I've worked here and my family was here, no one ever saw ghosts. Course that other crazy girl said she heard footsteps up on the third floor."

"Really?" Helen had heard things too?

The older woman put bread into the toaster. "No one believed her. She just wanted Mr. Mack to let her live in the garage. That girl was always saying silly things. She thought someone was readin' her email or goin' through her stuff. I mean, who would do that? Why?"

She thought about Helen's letters. Why had her friend been frightened? Ghosts didn't read email.

Peg stepped through the door from the dining room and nodded at Stacey. She poured a cup of coffee and turned to Mrs. D. "No need to cook dinner, Mary. I'm going to make stew tonight from the leftover pot roast."

"I didn't see any meat in the refrigerator," Mrs.

Delaney said, dishing up Stacey's eggs.

"I put it in there myself." Peg gave her a hard look and walked to the refrigerator. Mrs. D buttered the toast and brought the plate to Stacey.

She scooped eggs onto her toast and took a big bite, savoring the hint of herbs Mrs. D used. Thanks to Del's work in the garden the herbs were always fresh. She jumped, nearly dropping her toast as the refrigerator door slammed.

"I can't find the pot roast," Peg said in a high angry voice, turning to Mrs. D. "Did you make sandwiches for Mack last night?"

The older woman shook her head. "I never saw it, and Joe wouldn't touch anything in there without permission. Neither would Del."

Peg whirled to Stacey. "I don't mind if you eat anything out of the refrigerator. Certainly you might ask, but..."

Stacey licked her lips as two pairs of hard eyes zeroed in on her. "I didn't do it!"

"I won't fire you," Peg said. "All I ask is honesty."

"I didn't eat it."

"Aren't you the one who hears things in the night?"

Had she heard anything the night before? Only the normal creaks above her, but she shook her head.

"Maybe it was ghosts," Mrs. Delaney said with a harsh laugh.

Peg sighed heavily and rolled her eyes. "I don't mind sharing things. But there's one thing I hate and that's a liar." She marched out of the kitchen without waiting for an answer.

Stacey could only stare after her. "I didn't lie," she said in soft protest.

Mrs. D. shrugged. "Don't worry. She blows hot and cold. She won't remember the fight by lunch time."

Stacey pushed away her tasty eggs. Suddenly they weren't appetizing.

****

With the tension between her and Peg and her growing infatuation with Mack, Stacey didn't even mind when Carlos stopped in for another visit. At least he added humor to the house.

Thinking the two men were tied up in Mack's study, Stacey relaxed in the afternoon sun on the patio. She wanted to tackle another drawing of the house from a different angle.

She had just started when Carlos dropped onto the lounger beside her. "Mack says you're quite an artist. Is that why Peg is jealous of you?"

She continued working, though she wanted to ignore his sarcastic comment. She had a feeling he had made it to see her reaction. "Who says she's jealous?"

"One hears things. Or maybe Mack's taken a shine to you and Peg senses her days as his caretaker are numbered?"

"That's not funny," she protested, but it might explain why Peg had grown so cold. Stacey didn't believe it, though. She might be smitten, but in front of Peg, Mack had never indicated he saw her as anything other than his assistant. "I have a boyfriend, remember? I'm not a better artist either."

"Kenny says you are. He told me you're writing a cartoon together. When are you going to draw me? You can even make me the villain."

She glanced at him. Actually his lean, lined face presented an interesting challenge. She flipped over a page and began outlining him.

"How's the project going?" he asked, leaning back as though he knew what she was doing.

"Fine. You were right when you said Mack is in love with Lily. He's seeing only the good side of her.

He doesn't want to admit there was a dark side that might have thrown her into Greenlee's path."

His laugh was quick. "So you think there are dark secrets to our angel?"

"Perhaps. But he doesn't want to dig deeper."

"Mack spent years investigating the dark side of humanity. Part of him still wants to do that, but another part wants to find goodness in Lily."

"I don't know why. He's ignoring the drugs, the wild parties, the hosts of boyfriends. He's making her sound like a girl who lost her way, but lots of women accused her of trying to steal their boyfriends. I wonder if she didn't try to steal Ray Gibson from Mrs. D's sister. The picture of Lily Feeney in Helen Stanton's interviews is very different from the woman Mack is portraying in his writing."

"Very astute, young one. If only I was thirty years younger..." he said with a laugh.

"I thought you liked them young," she said with a smile.

"Only in years."

She jerked her head up. "What does that mean?"

"Lily was young, but not in years. Not like you. You see the world through that cartoon character of yours. Black and white. Right and wrong."

His words reminded her of what Helen had once said. She shook that off. "What about Lily? Do you think she saw it in gray?"

"A very dark gray, maybe all black. That's what Mack refuses to see."

"I understand that. This place is spooky. Some days there's no color but gray."

"And you're light," he said with a sly grin. "Peaches and sunshine."

Stacey didn't reply. She finished drawing and handed him the picture. His face held a scowl and he resembled a feral animal, menacing, waiting for victims.

"Oh, hell. You made me look old."

"I made you look your age."

Carlos laughed and pulled out his wallet. He dug through it to retrieve a card that he handed to her. "My original press card. I keep it for memories."

The picture was slightly cracked with age, but the old Carlos came through clearly. His jaw was pointed, his cheeks thin and angular. Even his nose looked sharper. His hair was jet black and fell in thick curls to his shoulders.

"Very 70's," she said.

"Very," he agreed. "I was a hungry kid looking for work and trouble. Now I look like a damned grandfather."

She took the card from him and began drawing again. After a few minutes she held up the sketch book. "What do you think?"

"Much better. Let me see that."

She handed him the book and he studied it as she sharpened her pencils.

"This is very good," he said and she looked up. He had flipped over a couple of pages. "You've got a good eye for detail. The house looks very forbidding, and you've really captured Mack. Imperious lord of the manor."

She grimaced, studying the drawing of Mack. "I did that the first day I was here. He scared me. Now I might draw him a little softer." Luckily her most recent pictures of Mack were kept in a small separate sketchbook she kept hidden under her bed.

He shook his head. "This is the Mack I used to know, the hard, cocky reporter who didn't care who he hurt to get a story. That's why this fascination with the good side of Lily is so wrong. You should draw her from one of the tabloids where she was cussing out photographers." He flipped back another page. "Something you want to tell me?"

"What?" She started to laugh, but then her skin began to crawl as she saw the sketch of her and Helen. She feigned a smile, though her heart was pounding and she feared it was so loud he could hear it. He was not Kenny; he would not accept an explanation that it was her imagination. "I drew that as a...I don't know...the two of us doing this job, you know."

"Except you said you drew Mack the first day? When did you draw this? Before that?"

She realized her error, but couldn't back down. "Right after I got the job. It's supposed to be symbolic. Old and the new?" At least that sounded good. A half truth concealed in honesty.

"How did you know what Helen Stanton looked like?"

"Her picture was in the paper."

He gazed at her for a minute, and her heart thudded. Did he guess? He closed the book and handed it back to her as he got to his feet. "You are a good artist. No wonder Peg's jealous. Let me give you a warning. If I were you, I'd be very careful. No one except Peg knows the truth about what happened to Mack's first two assistants. And there may be secrets about Helen too."

Stacey's hands shook as she watched Carlos lope back toward the house. Suddenly she needed to be away from Redfern Manor, even if she had to walk. She put her sketchbook on the table and walked to the edge of the grass and took the first path she found. What was he saying? That Peg had gotten rid of Mack's first assistants? How? Had she grown jealous of Helen too? Could she be dangerous if she was threatened?

Concerns about Peg weren't all that bothered Stacey though. She had come close to giving her identity away with the Helen picture. He'd studied it as though looking for a way to refute her comments.

Would he tell Mack? She stopped as she saw the freshly painted sign, reading "Danger: Quarry." An arrow pointed to the left.

With a quick twist, she turned in the other direction. The scent of dampness overwhelmed her as the mossy path muffled the sound of her footsteps. She was about to turn back when she saw a piece of fabric stuck to a tree. The bright yellow was familiar. It came from Helen's favorite sweater. She reached over and touched it. Her friend had been here! Didn't Del say she never walked in this direction?

She peered around the area in case there was other evidence of Helen. Branches from the tree had been broken as though something had pressed against them and the ground appeared trampled with much of the underbrush disturbed. She stepped forward and nearly choked. Like a light flashing on, the sun had poked through the trees, making something on the ground sparkle. She reached for it, knowing what it was even before the silver ID bracelet came loose from the overgrown brush. She turned it over, knowing the name plate would carry an engraving of a tiny Chinese symbol for Joy. She'd been with Helen when she bought it at a Chinese jewelry store in Portland.

How had Helen lost it? She considered it her good luck charm. Tears clouded Stacey's eyes. Her friend's luck had run out after she lost this bracelet.

As Stacey rose, she heard something. What? A crackling of a twig? Footsteps? She stayed silent, listening. Another crackle. What was that? An animal? Someone watching her? Slowly she rose to her feet, looking down as she concentrated on sounds in the forest.

As she stared down, she realized she was seeing something besides twigs and shrubbery. There was something else silvery under the leaves. She reached down and pushed them aside. Her breath caught and she picked up a small bright green and silver flash drive. Could this be Helen's missing notes?

She held it up triumphantly. The sound of cracking branches was close by and she began running back along the path. The crackling grew closer and she kept running. From behind something barreled into her like a lineman exploding through a pass rush in football. She crashed into a tree, her head banging against it hard and she literally saw stars as she tumbled to her knees. The flash drive flew out of her hand and something swept by her and then was gone.

It happened so fast she wasn't sure what had just happened. Dazed she rose to her feet and stumbled forward. Too late she realized she had run beyond the path that would take her to the house. She had gone too far and found herself teetering on the edge of the quarry again. She lurched back, grabbing at a tree, but its branches were slick and wet.

A heavy force smacked her from behind again and she toppled toward the edge. This time there was no grasping hand to catch her and she slid over the edge, falling for a few feet before something unknown broke her fall. It yanked her arm and jerked her to a stop, sending her crashing against the earthen wall. She flailed her legs in the air until they touched a narrow shelf. As she steadied herself, she discovered she was on a small ledge, anchored by a tree that was growing out of the side of the quarry. Helen's bracelet had caught on one of the branches and stopped her fall, jerking her against the side of the quarry. Above her, mud clods and pebbles rained down, pounding her head. Was someone up there? Could the person see her or had the culprit thought she had fallen all the way down. Someone had shoved her. She was sure of that. Who? Why? Her muscles ached but she pressed herself against the stone wall. Below her was a pool of water and mud, broken only by the jagged points of rock. If she fell, she would be hurt, maybe killed. Is that what the person above wanted?

Why? Del might not like her, but he didn't seem like the type who would be violent. Joe was strong enough, but she felt like she was making friends with him. Carlos liked to tease her, but hardly hated her.

What made her so sure it was a man? What about Mrs. Delaney? Or Peg? Could Peg be so jealous of her that she wanted her gone?

A sudden thought gripped Stacey as she had clutched the ledge. Had she discovered something about Helen that put her own life at risk? She thought about the strand from the yellow sweater and the flash drive by the rock. The flash drive! What had happened to it? It had flown from her hand during the initial attack.

Was the person who pushed her still up there? She longed to call out, but feared the person might come down to finish the job. Minutes crawled by. She tried pulling herself up the wall, but slid back onto the ledge. Only her grip on the tree kept her from sliding down the side of the quarry. How would she ever get up from this?

The afternoon was growing late and then dark. Surely someone would come looking for her. Her legs were growing weak from standing and pressing herself against the wall. How long could she hold on? Her knees were growing wobbly when she heard a voice.

"Stacey?"

Mack! But was he there to save her or to send her tumbling down the side? She'd avoided thinking about his motives for being rid of her.

"Stacey?"

That was Carlos calling, and then at a greater distance, she heard Del's voice.

They couldn't all want her dead.

"Over here," she cried as loud as she could

Moments later a flashlight appeared at the top.

"I'm down here," she called. Within minutes, a rope appeared and then Joe was beside her. With his assistance, she was able to climb along the rope to the top.

Mack caught her hand at the top and pulled her up, grasping her tightly. "Are you okay?"

She nodded but stumbled against him.

He lifted her into his arms and started to walk away from the quarry. After a few steps he faltered, and Carlos pulled her away from him.

"Damn fool," he muttered, though she didn't know if he meant her or Mack. Carlos carried her most of the way back to the house before she was finally able to walk on her own.

Peg greeted her at the door along with Mrs. Delaney. They muttered words of comfort when they heard where she'd been found, but Stacey noted that she saw no friendliness in the eyes of either woman. Peg's brow pinched in an accusing frown, while Mrs. D's colorless face remained rigid and stoic.

"She's freezing," Peg said in a curt tone. "We should get her into a bathtub. Mack, we'll use yours."

"You should probably take her to the hospital," Mrs. Delaney urged.

"I'm okay," Stacey protested, wanting to wave them all away. "There's no need for a hospital. I'm just cold." Her body ached, while her limbs shook. Or maybe it was the terror she had faced on that ledge, fearing any move would send her plummeting into the quarry.

Holding an arm around her shoulders, Carlos assisted her upstairs. Stacey perched on the edge of the toilet while Peg ran her bath. Mack had followed them, but he stood near the door, remaining silent. Stacey could feel his eyes on her, but she didn't look up. She was afraid to see what might be in his gaze. Condemning, like Peg? Indifferent, like Mrs. D? She didn't want to know.

Finally they retreated and Peg closed the door. Stacey stripped off her damp clothes and sank into the large tub, thinking about the first day she'd been in this bathroom, when she had been almost this cold. If only she'd known then what lay ahead.

She drank in the scent of lime soap and thought of Mack and while it sent a quick shiver through her body, it also ignited a warm sensation inside her. Slowly the inner glow of her thoughts and the hot water began to soothe her body. She stretched her muscles feeling the aches leaving them. If only she could as easily erase the cold dread that was growing inside her brain. Who had pushed her?

When she lifted herself from the tub and put on a soft terry robe left by Peg, Stacey almost expected to find Mack waiting in his bedroom. Or maybe that was what she'd hoped would happen. The large, orderly room was as empty and cold as the first day she walked into it, and she swallowed her disappointment. They had come a long way since that initial afternoon. Thinking about his eyes on her and their warm kiss, she shivered, but it was from female delight, not the cold.

At the edge of the bedroom, the door to his study was open and she approached it. Mack bent over his papers on his desk. He appeared to be deep in thought as he considered the pages.

"Mack?"

He started and shoved the papers into a nearby folder before whirling around. His blue eyes met hers and she was pleased to see they carried concern and something else. What? Or maybe it wasn't concern—perhaps it was irritation at her ongoing stupidity. Then a soft smile curved his full lips upward and she felt her insides melt. Any traces of her earlier frigidity fell away.

"Come in," he said in a gentle tone that soothed her even more. He inclined his head toward the desk. "How are you feeling?"

She hesitated at the door before stepping into the room. "I...I'm fine."

"I'm pleased to see you're getting some of your color back," he said with a nod. "You had me scared. You had us all scared."

She touched her warm cheeks. They were probably very bright right now. How much could she tell him? Did she trust him or had he done it? No, his blue eyes were filled with apprehension. "I scared myself," she said softly.

"I thought you realized how dangerous that trail is. You went right past the signs Del put up. Were you lost?"

"Not this time. Someone pushed me down," she blurted.

He straightened in his chair and a frown slashed his face. "How could that be?"

She had no answer and he rose and held out his hand toward her. "Please, Stacey, come here for a minute. Let's talk."

He drew her to a small loveseat along one wall of the office. Unlike the parlor downstairs, this room was neat and organized as his bedroom. Bookcases lined one wall and a large desk that matched the one downstairs sat in front of them. But this room also had several comfortable chairs in addition to the love seat.

"You had a hell of a fall. Would you like a shot of brandy or something?" he asked.

"I would like someone to listen to me. I didn't fall. Someone pushed me."

Chapter Eight

A nerve in Mack's jaw twitched as he studied her. She could read the skepticism in his clear sapphire eyes. He ran his hand through his short sandy hair, a gesture she recognized as frustration. Perhaps this was not the time to push this.

"I'm sorry for frightening everyone," she said, keeping her voice calm and even. She pressed her lips together, fighting to stifle the words she wanted to blurt out about the person who had pushed her. "Thank you for coming to look for me."

He attempted a smile as he dropped himself onto the sofa beside her. He reached over and pushed her damp hair from her face. "I knew you had to be around here. Dependable little Stacey. You're never far away."

She didn't feel dependable, and his touch sent a torch of heat racing across her cheek. Her lips trembled as she let her true feelings spill out. "I was so scared... I didn't know how long I could hold on."

His fingers grazed her chin, lifting it. She realized he was using his right hand and she touched it.

"Your right hand," she said. "You used it to lift me up."

"There's nothing that's really wrong with the strength in my hand," he admitted. "I don't use it much because its movement is awkward and I suppose I'm vain about it. According to my doctor the physical therapy we've been doing in the gym has helped, and I have you to thank for that." He leaned toward her and she closed her eyes, hoping he meant to kiss her again.

A quick knock on the door froze them both for an instant. Mack drew back and rose to his feet. "Yes?"

The door opened Carlos stuck his head inside. "How's our girl?"

Mack gestured at where Stacey remained sitting on the sofa and then stepped away from her as Carlos entered the room, followed by Peg.

"Stacey, you're out of the tub." A frown crossed her face as her sharp gaze traveled from Stacey to Mack. "Are you hungry? I put a sandwich in your room. Come, I'll walk you there and sit with you while you eat it. You need to get to bed."

****

Stacey wasn't certain what she expected after her harrowing adventure. If she'd thought someone from the house had pushed her, she discovered she might be right. Suddenly everyone seemed to want to be rid of her. Mrs. D shoved her coffee at her the next morning, and even the eggs tasted dry.

"Maybe you ought to tell the Warrens to get a new girl."

"What?" Stacey jerked her head up to stare at the woman whose voice had grown cold and unfriendly.

For a minute her withered face softened. "You're a nice girl, Stacey. I'd hate to see you end up like those others."

Stacey thought about what Carlos had said about Mack's first assistants. "The other assistants, did they end up like Helen? Dead?"

The woman leveled a cool look at her. "No. But one girl gave up her job and came all the way out here just to get fired by Miz Warren after a week. And the other, well, she just up and took off. And then that Stanton girl dying. I don't know. Maybe this job is cursed."

Stacey couldn't even joke about being a jinx. She

could see Mrs. D was serious.

Luckily Del came stomping into the house at that point, but he was just as sour, not even inquiring if she was okay. "You want me to take you into town? I hear your car is ready. Maybe you can go home now." His tone made it obvious he meant home to wherever she'd come from.

She saw him exchange a knowing look with Mrs. D. Did they all want her to leave? Why?

Stacey pressed her lips together firmly, just as determined not to give in to whoever had tried to hurt her. "Thank you, but I need to catch up on my work since I was gone yesterday."

"I'm not going until this afternoon. I just took Carlos and Mr. Mack to catch the early ferry."

"Mack is gone?" she asked in surprise. "He didn't tell me he was going anywhere."

"He's the boss. He doesn't need to tell you," Peg said from the door. She stepped into the room, regal as a queen bee in a gray sweater and matching knit slacks. "But I doubt it means you can have the day off. He said something before he left about leaving dictation he needed done. It's probably in his room."

Stacey shoved aside her half eaten eggs. So much for everyone worrying about her close brush with death. Maybe the men in town were right. This was a cold bunch.

****

The click of Mack's door seemed to reverberate in the hall. Stacey made a face. It shouldn't matter. Mack was gone and she had Peg's permission to go into his study, right?

And she'd been in there at his invitation the previous night. Had he meant to kiss her? The thought still made her feel warm inside.

Stacey entered on tiptoes as though someone might be listening. She crossed to his desk and then paused as a slash of sunlight came from the turret.

"Wow," she whispered. The rays filled the octagonal room with slivers of sunlight through a ring of stained glass that surrounded the top edges of the windows. She let out a cry and stepped into the room. The view was as magnificent as that from Lily's room. Damn! If only she had her watercolors. Maybe she should go into town with Del and pick some up. Maybe even some paint. One way or another she was going to paint this amazing view. If only she could capture the way the sun poured through those stained glass windows!

She turned away from the view. She needed to get to work, but maybe... Mack was gone. Stepping lightly, but with determination, Stacey hurried across the hall and grabbed her sketch pad.

****

Stacey wanted to share the drawings she made while sitting in Mack's office, but given his warnings about visiting there, she kept them to herself. She spent the afternoon in his office, not leaving until she heard Peg come up the stairs.

As they sat in the drawing room after dinner, she was still thinking about how to get him to let her to return. He'd asked her to stay for a drink because he wanted to talk to her. She could tell Mack had something on his mind, but he gave no indication as he poured a glass of tawny port for them both.

His opening remark surprised her. "My sister thinks I'm burying myself here and I should get out more. Maybe even think of trying to get married again. What do you think?"

"It has to be up to you," Stacey said, her throat growing dry. The drawing room was cool despite the fire that crackled in the stone fireplace. She hadn't seen him all day, not since the night before when he'd been so sweet about her close brush with the quarry. Was he feeling guilty for not believing her claim that someone pushed her? Or was Carlos right and was Peg trying to push Mack away from her?

He stared into the golden liquid of his drink, as though it might hold the answer. "She has it in her mind, no one can be happy alone. She thinks if I remarry it'll improve my disposition."

"She's alone," Stacey pointed out. She stopped short of adding maybe marriage would improve Peg's cold attitude.

"Hmmpf. That's different. She says she chooses to be alone." He held up a finger, waving it as though using it to punctuate the word "choosing."

Stacey stared at the left hand he'd held up. He was no longer wearing his wedding band. "Aren't...you...um...sort of choosing to be alone?" she stammered, flustered by the sight of his bare finger. Her stomach churned. What would she do if he began dating, bringing different women to the house? Could she stand to watch him fall in love? A tiny pang of pain ripped at her stomach.

"Yeah, true," he said in more of a grunt than a reply.

She sipped her port, aware her breath had started to come in quick shallow gasps. There was something intimate about being in this dimly lit room with him, the fire crackling in the grate. Outside rain pelted the windows and the wind had picked up, rattling the windows. They had never really discussed personal lives to this level—not about dating or getting involved.

"You've been working damn hard," he said, suddenly changing the subject. "Thanks for finishing up those pages. I didn't mean for you to work today."

She bit her tongue to keep from telling him Peg had practically ordered her to work. She also didn't reveal the hours she spent in the turret with her sketchpad. "I didn't mind. I needed to keep busy."

"What will you do when we're finished with this project?"

She hadn't thought that far ahead. Did he want her gone too? Like Mrs. D and Del?

"I suppose I'll go back to looking for work as a commercial artist. Sooner or later someone will hire me."

"Check with Peg. She might know some people."

"Maybe," she said, though given Peg's overall unhappiness with her, she doubted that.

"If you're worried about me, Mack, please don't. I really can take care of myself."

"Even if you can't tell left from right?" he asked, but for once he was smiling, a tiny gleam dancing in his eyes, or maybe it was the glow from the fire. "It isn't difficult to fix, you know. I thought about this the other day. I've noticed you don't wear a watch. Maybe if you put one on your left hand, you'd have an easier time figuring it out."

Stacey had kept Helen's bracelet in her pocket all day. Now she fingered it. "That's a great idea. Maybe...a bracelet."

"Exactly."

She burst into laughter. "That's so simple." It was even more fitting that she could use Helen's bracelet. It would be like having her friend with her all the time.

He lifted a finger. "So problem one solved." He moved toward her and her breath caught as he stopped very close to her. "Now there is problem number two."

She inhaled sharply as he sat beside her. Close. So close she could smell the wonderful scent of his lime soap. "Problem..." she began.

He nodded, his face moving closer to her. "I think we both know what that is. Running from it won't help either one of us."

Her breath had become shallow again and now her fingers shook. Her insides no longer churned at the thought of him with someone else. They grew warm and the tingling sensations he normally gave her turned into outright quaking, like the walls of her insides were hot and crumbling.

"Don't say you haven't been thinking about this since that other night," he said as his fingers brushed her hair. "It's been on my mind at least once a day since the first time we kissed."

She could hardly breathe and her clothes seemed very tight. The ends of her fingers tingled with wanting to touch him as her lower body began to smolder and not from the sherry. He'd been thinking of her since that kiss too? She felt as warm and limp as a wet bath towel.

"I saw the look in your eyes that night. And I know what I felt. That jolt was not one sided. I could sense your reaction and I've seen the flush in your cheeks when we're close. I know how I feel every time you're around me. I can feel it all the way to my toes sometimes just looking at you." He leaned toward her, burrowing his face into her neck, inhaling sharply. The touch sent shivers of hot desire, of growing need through her trembling body. His lips were warm against her sensitive skin as his tongue flicked out to taste her neck.

"Umm," he groaned deep in his throat. "You taste like honey, so sweet."

Stacey's body shuddered, as his hands spanned her abdomen, drawing wide circles with his palms. She shook again and wrapped her arms around his neck, feeling his crisp hair in her fingers. His lips trailed up her neck, across her hot cheeks and then found her mouth. They touched her lips quickly. And then again. She opened her mouth to his and drank in his touch, his tongue thrusting inside to explore her mouth. His shoulders and chest were hard against her searching hands and she felt like she was melting against him. The scent of his lime soap assaulted her, much as it had the previous night in his tub. But this was the heat from his body, not the water this time.

Their kiss grew more passionate and he slid his hands under her shirt, up to dip the tops of his fingers into her bra. Her nipples were large and hard and she quivered with wanting him.

She wanted him so badly she ached inside. Her breasts seemed to thrust themselves into his hands as his fingers undid the front clasp to free them. Her quick tremble made him groan deep in his throat. His touch was magic, as though he knew exactly how to arouse her. But she didn't need much. Stacey was a virtual fire, waiting for him to consume her.

He lifted his lips from hers moving to her ear, whispering. "I want you, Stacey. I want you so damn bad."

She slid her arms under his sweater touching the skin of his chest, his back feeling the edges of his scars and wishing she could heal his insides as they had healed. "Me too, Mack," she admitted. "I've been wanting you…"

Her lower body became molten, pained with wanting him inside her. He kissed her again, their tongues dancing together, exploring and thrusting as though he was already inside her. They were both breathless as he broke the kiss and held her close to him.

"I'm sorry. I'm sorry. I keep fighting this."

"Then don't," she urged his lips before moving hers to explore his ear and nibble on the lobe. She'd never felt so forward before, as though she wanted to devour a man or have him devour her.

He pulled back with a slight moan and opened her blouse and gazed down at her breasts. She could see the flames of desire in his eyes and it only made her shiver more.

"I want you," he said. "But not here." He drew a deep breath and shut his eyes and then closed her blouse. "And unfortunately, not like this."

Instead of feeling warm as the night air was cut off from her skin, she felt cold. "What? Why?"

He lurched away from her, turning and picking up his drink and downing it. He looked back at her and Stacey realized her blouse had fallen open. But she wanted him to see her. She wanted to see that fiery look in his eyes again.

"I know you have a boyfriend..."

"What? Boyfriend?"

"Carlos told me." She leaned back against the couch. Damn Carlos for telling him. She didn't want Phil. She wanted Mack. She'd never felt like she wanted a man before. She had spent many weekends with Phil, but he'd never ignited sparks like Mack could. He had never sent hot fires burning through her.

"It's over with Phil," she admitted.

He held up his hand. "You say that now, tonight in front of a fire, but we need to think about tomorrow. That's what I keep thinking about."

She inhaled sharply. How could she make him understand it had been over even before this night? But she had not given that impression to Carlos. She had lied to him. Did she want to admit to Mack that she had lied?

"So now what?" she asked.

He turned away from her. "To be honest, I don't know. I guess we both need to think. We need to get through this work and then...then...talk."

"Or kiss?" she asked, her fingers touching her lips that had grown wildly sensitive.

His laugh was quick and harsh. "Something like that. I guess I see you as living in that pretend world you build with Kenny. Everything is fiction and fun and no one really gets hurt." He shook his head. "I see the real side. The pain. Even you can't hide that, and I don't want you to feel that pain. Like Lily."

Lily. Of course. That was what was behind this all. Maybe that damn ghost was even behind his thoughts about her. He was right. If they made love, then what? What would Mack expect of her? Brief moments of passion? He wasn't in love with her. He was probably thinking of that damn first meeting— her body. And that comparison he had once made of her thoughts to Lily's as they stood in Lily's room that day they'd visited it.

Lily. That was who was really between them. He might have stopped wearing his wedding band, but how could she compete with the ghost of that damn Lily Feeney? She could become his physical lover, but would he ever see her as anything but the woman he really wanted?

She began to button her blouse. "I better go to bed. We have a lot of work to do."

He moved toward her and caught her hand. "You can see that I'm right. A personal relationship would spoil what we have going. I want you to think. Seriously. And maybe when we're finished, we can talk again." He dropped her hand and turned away.

Stacey walked to the door on shaking legs. They were every bit as wobbly as when she'd fallen into the quarry. At the door she stopped. "Mack, one thing... It really is over with Phil. I thought it was over before I got here, but I'm really sure about it now." She turned and hurried out the door before he could reply.

Chapter Nine

"Say, Miss?" Del appeared at the door to the gym as Stacey finished working with Joe. To her surprise Mack had not appeared that morning. Maybe he'd slept in after being gone all day with Carlos. Or maybe he didn't want to face her after their intimate evening.

Stacey walked over to greet Del. "Good morning."

"What about your car?" he asked in a grumpy tone, without returning her greeting. "They called me again. It's ready to be picked up."

Oh, rats. She had forgotten all about his telling her that the previous day. "Thanks for reminding me"

"If you need a ride to pick it up, let me know. My cousin's working down at the shop and he said there wasn't much wrong with it, so don't let Bodie try to scam you into paying more."

"Thanks for letting me know."

Given her bad times with Mack and Peg, Stacey knew she couldn't afford to ask for time off, but she would like to pick up her car. And she didn't want to wait to ask Mack.

"Maybe after breakfast?"

"Sure. Just let me know."

She watched him shuffle away and thought about whether she should trust him to drive her into town. Ever since her close brush she'd been studying everyone closely, but she was having a difficult time thinking Del might be the culprit. While he and Mrs. D had seemed to want her to leave, he had become nicer to her in the past two weeks. She'd taken coffee to him several times and offered to help him start transferring plants from the greenhouse to flower beds along the veranda.

She tossed down her gloves and looked at Joe who was eyeing her from across the gym. She couldn't imagine why he'd want to hurt her. In some ways she felt like they had bonded during their kick boxing lessons.

She wasn't even sure about Mrs. D as she sat down to breakfast and told him about Del taking her into town.

"Can I get a sweet roll for him?" she asked.

"You're going to spoil the old coot," Mrs. D said with a frown.

"Like I haven't seen you take him the left over breakfast rolls," Stacey teased.

"Someone's got to eat 'em."

"I think he likes you," Stacey teased.

Mrs. D. stopped rolling dough for bread and gave Stacey a fierce look, but to her surprise the woman blushed. "Don't be silly."

Stacey still hadn't figured out whether Mrs. D would have wanted to hurt her. She seemed to be pushing her to quit, but as she stared at the blush spreading on the woman's face, she doubted that Mrs. D could hurt anyone. That flush was so familiar—a woman who was interested in a man. Was she interested in Del? Stacey stifled a giggle at her protest.

"He always sees that you get the prettiest flowers for the kitchen and dining room. And he takes special care with the herb garden. You think he does that for Peg?"

"You are a silly girl," she said, but now a slight smile tugged at the corner of her lips.

Stacey left the kitchen laughing. Why did this place have to be cursed? Why had someone tried to get rid of her? She was starting to think she wanted to stay. She was growing used to the old house and its creaks. She might even be getting used to Mrs. D and Del and their quirks. And then there was Mack....

She shook her head. She didn't want to think about him. The night before Kendra had truly fallen in love with her cartoon hero and before going to bed, Stacey had drawn another sketch of Mack. Hopefully he never saw it because she feared it showed her true feelings about him. Could he have wanted to hurt her? No, not after the way he'd kissed her. He had admitted wanting her. And she more than wanted him. She knew now she was in love with him. Totally, fully, and more than she could ever imagine wanting or loving anyone. He might not love her—yet, but was there a chance she could teach him to love again? She wanted that more than anything. At least she knew he was not the person out to get her.

So that left Carlos and Peg. Actually it left Peg as the most likely assailant. Carlos had nothing against her. He seemed to find her amusing, and he even hinted she might help Mack out of his depression. Was he concerned because of that drawing he'd seen of her and Helen? He'd never mentioned it before he left Evergreen Island. Wouldn't he have told Mack the truth if he wanted to be rid of her? Why push her off a cliff?

Back to Peg. Had she hurt Mack's old assistants out of jealousy? Had she tried to get rid of Helen but Helen had fought back? Or had Helen—like her—decided she wanted to stay?

There was no way of knowing. Maybe Del could help with answers and she decided to run through her list of possible suspects with him and see if she could figure anything out. She started with Mary Delaney.

He appeared not to notice what she was doing, but then she was always asking questions. "Nice woman. Lost her husband in the war when Kenny was just a baby.

"Do you ever see her socially?"

"Huh?"

"Have you ever taken her out?"

He gave her a quick look of disbelief. "Why would she wanna go any place with me?"

"Why not? You ought to take her for dinner at the Gull's Roost or something." She couldn't imagine Mary Delaney wanting to go to the formal French restaurant in town.

He chuckled suddenly, surprising her. "Well, hell's bells. What are you doing? Playing matchmaker?"

"Why not?"

He looked over at her and shook his head. "Let me give you a piece of advice. After we pick up your car today, if I was you I wouldn't worry about me and Mary. I'd drive back to that house and give Mack Warren your letter of resignation and be on the next ferry out of here."

"Why?"

All traces of good humor were gone from his face as he studied her. "Because I don't think Helen Stanton jumped off that cliff. I can't prove it, but I'd hate to see you found the same way. And don't ask me to explain any of that, because I can't. Except you and I both know it's true."

****

Stacey barely listened to the explanation of what was wrong with her car. She was too fascinated by the lean blonde man who stood behind Bodie Lewis. Slim, lean and still handsome though he was over fifty, Ray Gibson didn't resemble a convict. He looked more like a Hollywood leading man, playing the role of a mechanic—except for the tattoos that ran up the side of his arms and peeked out from the neckline of his t-shirt.

"Can I talk to you?" she asked after signing the bill for her car and Bodie Lewis told him to take her to it.

"About what?"

"Did you talk to Helen Stanton?"

He stopped, standing in a defensive stance, faded green eyes wary. "Why do you care?"

"I replaced her."

"Yeah, so?"

"Well, I looked through her notes and I saw that she wanted to talk to you about Lily Feeney."

His grunt was cold. "Too bad. It's not like Warren is telling the truth anyway."

"What do you mean?"

"Look, I talked to him. His questions were different than hers. She wanted to know about LA and all that crap. I talked to him a long time ago while I was in jail and what he wanted to know was about the stuff here when we were in high school. He wanted me to talk about what a sweet kid she was. He don't want to know about her life once she left and what she did in Hollywood."

Stacey knew that, but she didn't correct him. "He's trying to get an overall picture..."

"Uh-uh. He's painting a picture of some perfect angel. Not Lily and not what she wanted to be. I was with her for two weeks and I found out the truth. The real truth. Not that pretty picture. And you don't want to know the truth."

"So you think she fit into that profile of the girls Kevin Greenlee killed."

"Totally, but I don't think he killed her. I think one of those guys she hung out with and cheated on killed her."

Stacey gulped, chills running through her. While she had read as much in Helen's notes, she was talking to someone who had been there. Who might know the truth. "Why do you say that?"

"Because I was with her. I coulda killed her." He turned and walked away and Stacey stared after him. She pulled her coat tightly around her as she slid into her car and turned on the heat full blast.

****

Stacey started back toward Redfern Manor but then pulled into a parking space at the post office. There was no telling when she would be able to get back to town and check her mail. Not that she was expecting anything. She was surprised to see a notice for a package inside her box. The contents of the package were even more surprising.

A purple backpack slid out. The note from her mother was cryptic.

Here is that backpack you were looking for. It fell behind the bed. Might wanna clean when you come back. Also putting in another letter from Helen. Looks like she mailed it just before she died.

Stacey had not told her it was Helen's backpack, only that she needed to find it. Wonderful. Now what would she do with it? She'd have to send it to Helen's parents. She fingered the letter from Helen. Somehow she knew this was the final letter.

With shaking fingers she opened it.

Stace,

I wish you had come. I need your help and counsel now like never before. This has not turned out at all as I had hoped. I've stumbled into a mess and now I'm really scared I've discovered something meant to stay hidden. Mack Warren has uncovered a bees' nest and I don't know if he doesn't realize it or if he's hoping to hide it. There are times I think he'll do anything to hide the truth about Lily Feeney.

I don't know if it's his guilt because he was piloting the plane that killed his wife so he wants to write something good about this woman, but he's

120

building her into an unreal goddess that he worships. It scares me. And I fear he might even hurt me if I try to tell the truth about Lily. I want out, but I don't see how it can happen.

Please come. Please help me. You've always been my rock. I need you now. Bring the backpack. It has all the answers.

H

Fear invaded Stacey. Had Helen discovered the truth about Lily so Mack had gotten rid of her? Had she been going in that same direction and was that why someone or maybe even Mack had pushed her off the cliff?

She undid the clip on the backpack and opened it, but she felt like she always knew what was inside. John Scotti's handwritten notes spilled out into the seat of the car. She fingered the scribbled notes. They didn't make much sense to her. She started to put them back into the folder they'd fallen out of and then saw the page of a black and white sketch. Hadn't one of Helen's notes said something about a composite?

She studied it. The lean face with the baseball cap was familiar. Ray in his twenties? Could Ray have killed Lily? Or was this a bad picture of Kevin Greenlee? She didn't even remember what the man looked like, but Mack would have pictures.

Should she go back to Redfern Manor? Her lips were dry and she feared she was going to choke, but Stacey could not just run away. She looked at the ferry terminal where a ferry was coming into port. Maybe she should follow Del's advice and go catch it when it boarded in half an hour.

Passengers began to spill from the decks and she watched them walk off. Bike riders and cars followed. For an instant as she watched the steady stream, she thought she was seeing things. A bearded man in a yellow slicker carrying a black back pack turned his bicycle toward the road that led toward Three Mile Walk. His loping gait reminded her of Carlos. No, Mack had put him on the ferry the previous day. Had gone into town with him. She was seeing things.

She turned away from the ferry, started her car and began driving away from the post office. What should she do? Call Mack from Anacortes when the ferry docked?

No, she had not helped Helen before. She needed to see this through. If someone had been responsible for her friend's death, she needed to find out who it was and see that justice was done.

Even if it was Mack? Was that what Helen's letter charged?

Stacey's mind raced as she drove back toward Redfern Manor. She had grown to love Mack. How could he be a killer? But women fell in love with killers all the time. It could happen. He said he cared about her, but he had often stated his disdain for Helen.

The rain began in earnest as she rounded the turn toward the house and it jumped out at her with its gargoyle ugliness. But it was no longer ugly to her. In some ways she was growing used to its split personality. It was almost like her and Kendra. She parked her car outside the garage and went up the back steps.

Mrs. D. looked up from stirring a pot on the stove, surprised to see her.

"I got my car back," Stacey said, waving her key ring.

She nodded. "You better get to work, girl. Mr. Mack's been screaming for you since he got up."

Stacey sighed. She should never have gone off without leaving him a note or telling Peg. She glanced at her watch. It was only 9:30. Heck, she was only an hour late and she could put in extra hours on the other end. And she'd worked the previous day when he was gone. Hadn't he told her the night before she didn't need to work?

Stacey walked to the parlor and was surprised to discover he wasn't there. She touched the intercom. "Mack?"

"Come up here," he ordered, his voice cold.

Yikes, that didn't sound good. He must really be upset that she'd just taken off. As she lifted the purple backpack, she realized she held a trump card. Wait until he heard about John Scotti's notes! How would she explain that? Maybe she should tell him she found it in an unopened box after his anger blew off. Picking up a box, she emptied the contents on a chair and deposited the backpack inside before heading upstairs. She knocked at his door and entered at his tense command.

"Hi, Mack, I'm sorry I've been gone..."

Stacey didn't know what she noticed first. His stricken face or the sketch he held in his tight fist. She could have sworn her heart stopped. The picture she'd drawn of her and Helen! Oh, hell, she'd left her sketchpad in the turret the previous day when she heard Peg coming upstairs. Instead she'd carried out dictation tapes and blank pieces of paper to pretend she'd been working.

He wielded the sketch book like a club. "Want to tell me about this?"

She licked her parched lips, but her tongue was just as dry. If she spoke, she'd swallow the damn thing.

"You knew Helen Stanton?" he asked, his voice rising.

"Well..." The answer she'd given Carlos stuck in her throat. She could never lie to Mack in a convincing fashion. There was no way out—except the truth. "Um...yes."

He blinked, his face growing stern in that way

she had come to recognize as being deep in thought. His eyes burrowed in on hers. "She was the friend you told me about, the one who died," he said through gritted teeth.

Her chest felt full, and she was barely able to breathe. "Yes."

Mack swiveled toward her, blue eyes flashing like warning signs. "Why?"

"What do you mean?"

"Why did you lie? Why did you come here? To find out about us? To find out if we drove her to suicide?"

"I didn't believe that she would commit suicide. Not Helen."

His mouth hung open, his eyes incredulous. "She was erratic those last days, despondent."

Tears edged into her eyes, but Stacey couldn't back down. Not about this. "Not Helen. She was scared."

"Of what?" he demanded. "She'd broken up with a boyfriend. She could barely function."

"Boyfriend? She didn't have a boyfriend," she protested.

"Really?" he asked, tilting his head to the side.

The definite way he said that frightened her. Had there been someone in Helen's life? She mentioned a man right after arriving on the island, but never talked about him again. For a time she thought it might be Mack, until she met him and discovered how he viewed Helen.

"She said he was coming to meet her at the ferry the day she died," Mack added.

A cold chill ran through her. "That...was me...I was..." she stopped. She couldn't admit she had failed to show up.

"Why would she lie?"

"Why would she commit suicide?" she retorted. "I grew up with Helen. She would never kill herself."

"Then you don't know about the note."

Stacey went cold inside. "The...note?"

"The note the sheriff found in her coat pocket. Saying everyone had turned against her. She no longer wanted to go on."

The words were not Helen. "Can I see it?"

"The sheriff has it," Mack said, "or he sent it to her folks. I don't know where it is."

Stacey sagged into the nearest chair. She'd never felt so horrible in her life. Had she really known Helen at the end? Had she let her down one more time in coming here? She bit down hard on her lip. She could feel Mack watching her as despair wracked her body. She wanted to cry, shout, but she didn't know about what.

She'd let Helen down again.

No. She had come.

She had the backpack.

As for the note, she looked up at Mack as a horrible thought ran through her. She had not heard about any damn note. How could he know about it?

"You know, you think you know Helen so well... You think she lied and that she lost John Scotti's notes that she never made a thumb drive for you. But you know what? She didn't lie! I saw that thumb drive when I was by the quarry the other day! And all of John Scotti's notes are in her backpack downstairs. I hid them in a box! They prove everything Helen was trying to tell you."

She wasn't certain about that last part, but as his face turned crimson, she found she couldn't stop herself. "You don't want to believe the truth about Helen any more than you want to believe the truth about Lily Feeney! She's a ghost that you're clinging to because you don't want to work at being whole again or getting over your injuries!"

Mack was bright red now and he looked ready to explode. Stacey knew she had gone too far and she ran from the room.

He called after her, but she hopped down the stairs, knowing he could never catch her before she got out of the house.

Chapter Ten

Once she was out the door, Stacey started to run toward her car, but as she fumbled in her pocket, she realized she'd left her keys in the kitchen. Fearing he'd catch her if she went back inside, she walked passed her car and behind the garage. She glanced around anxiously and then with her head down, she turned toward the trees. The wet grass was slippery but she barely felt it soaking through her shoes. She was not going to be frightened any more. Had Mack Warren pushed her friend off the cliff? How did he know about a suicide note if he hadn't written it?

Mack, though? Could he really have been that mercenary?

Part of her refused to accept that. She'd come to care about Mack, to love him. Could he hurt anyone? That man who kissed her so gently? Who aroused feelings in her she didn't know she had?

Tears streamed down her cheeks. She needed to keep a clear head.

What would Kendra do? Oh, the hell with Kendra! Stacey needed to make a plan. Maybe she needed to retrace her steps from her last trip to the woods and find that thumb drive. It would prove that Helen had come out to the woods and might have the proof about Lily too. Holding up her wrist to make certain she was going to the left, Stacey found she didn't need it. She knew where to go. Her eyes scanned the underbrush as she neared the spot where she'd been pushed into the quarry. She could see all the matted leaves and branches where she'd been pushed, but she saw no sign of the thumb drive.

She thought about going back to the house. What was Mack doing right now? Looking for her? No, probably searching frantically for the backpack. Lily and her secrets were all that mattered to him.

The crackle of breaking branches sent a trickle of fear down her spine. A black jacket appeared through the branches coming toward her. She breathed a sigh of relief when she saw Carlos, his head down.

"What are you doing here?" she asked, stepping toward him. "I thought you went back to Seattle. Did Mack send you to look for me while he looks for the backpack?"

He drew up and stared at her in surprise. "What backpack?"

"He saw my picture with Helen. He knows I knew her. Or did you tell him?"

Carlos studied her for a moment and then shook his head. "I admit I figured it out after you got so upset over that picture, but I never said anything. What's this backpack he's looking for? Helen's? It has the notes, right?"

"Yes, and I told him I had it so I'm sure he's looking for it. He's so damn busy protecting Lily and her reputation. It's like she rules him from beyond the grave."

His laugh was quick and sharp. "I warned you."

"But I don't think he killed Helen."

"What? You think Mack killed Helen to protect Lily? Why? How?"

"I know people think I'm clumsy and silly, but I know I didn't fall in the quarry and I know Helen wouldn't commit suicide. Someone pushed me and they probably killed her too. I'm looking for the thumb drive I dropped here the other day." She glanced around the area and then realized he'd been searching the ground when she saw him. Her breath caught as everything began to fall into place.

"Oh, no, it was you!" She waited for him to deny it, to laugh at her, but the dark serious look that crossed his feral face almost stopped her heart.

"I wondered how long it would take you to figure that out. Just like Helen, you're very smart and very thorough, but unlike her, you're not blinded by wild thoughts of romance. I thought of seducing you."

She shivered, recalling what Mack had said about Helen having a boyfriend. "Like you did with her? That would never have worked."

"I figured that out right away. You're like Lily was before she left here, believing in romance."

Another link in the chain fell into place as she thought about the face in the composite sketch. Suddenly she knew where she had seen it before—in her own sketchbook. "That's why you killed Helen. You...you killed Lily too! You were the other boyfriend. The one she used to fight with. I thought it was Ray, and probably Helen did at first too. But she saw that composite just like me. I didn't put it together until just now. It looks just like the picture I drew of your old press pass."

The shock that swept across his face would have given her a sense of triumph, if the circumstances weren't frightening. She was alone with a killer!

"Is that what did it? It never occurred to me that that's how she put it all together."

"You killed her here and took her to that other place."

"It wouldn't do to kill someone so close to home. I discovered that with Lily. I'd been to Greenlee's crime scenes so staging the body was no problem. No one would have put it together until Mack and John started digging. I knew they'd never let it go."

"You sabotaged Mack by getting rid of his assistants."

"Peg did that. I accused one of stealing so she fired her. Then I convinced the other girl Mack was unstable, so she took off. But Helen really got into this murder mystery thing. She wanted to prove Greenlee didn't do it."

"Why did you kill Lily?"

"It was an accident. She was such a damn flirt. Always some new guy who was going to be the man of her dreams. It was me, but she never saw it." He shuddered and shook his head.

"I knew Mack and John would eventually put it all together. I hoped once John was gone, Mack would drop the case."

Another horrifying thought struck her. "You killed John Scotti?"

"He always suspected Lily wasn't one of Greenlee's victims. He was drinking a lot and on so damn much medication it wasn't hard to give him an overdose. I guess whatever he took ended up looking like a heart attack. That was a damn lucky break because he'd started to re-interview people who knew Lily. People had seen me with her and I guess he had someone do that damn composite."

"You had me fooled about Helen. I even thought maybe Peg did it."

"Peg?" His laugh came out as more of a snort. "Why would Peg do it?"

"Well, you said she got jealous. So I thought maybe she was afraid Mack was falling for Helen and wanted to get rid of her. Maybe she wants to keep Mack to herself. She chooses to be alone, but I get the impression she doesn't like being out here all by herself."

"Don't be silly. Peg would love to see him get hitched again. She feels responsible for her baby bro, which is why she's here and so damn bitchy. She hates this place, but it's where he wants to be."

"Mack's going to find out the truth, you know.

Once he finds that backpack and sees the composite."

"Which is why I need to get rid of you and go find the damn thing myself. I thought I'd burned everything in the fire. Yesterday Mack tells me you've started finding pieces in some of the boxes and I saw you pick up a thumb drive the other day."

"So you came back. But you've been here all along, haven't you? In the house?"

He pointed a finger at her like a gun. "I knew you were smart."

"The figure by the garage. That was you. You've been living upstairs in Lily's room. Raiding the refrigerator at night."

"Bingo. It was easy to go up and down the back stairs. I just made a copy of the key."

"You tried to kill me because I was seeing and hearing things."

"No. I really didn't mean to hurt you. I wanted that thumb drive, and I know it's still around here somewhere. I hoped scaring you would make you quit and go home. I thought that's what you were doing at the ferry terminal today. But you came back."

"I don't give up, and Mack will never believe another suicide."

"No, so you'll get lost. Forever. Everyone knows you can't tell directions. What do you think?"

"Mack will find out the truth. He's consumed with Lily right now, but maybe later..."

"Then I'll worry about that later."

She considered her options. What could he do to her? She hadn't seen a weapon, but there were rocks and tree limbs around. He was stronger. It wouldn't take much to overpower her and get rid of her as he had Helen. What *would Kendra do?*

Fight! But she wasn't Kendra!

Wait! Who had gotten Kendra out of all those

131

jams?

She had!

But Kendra could kick and fight.

So could she! Stacey's heart raced. Somehow she was going to get out of this mess. "You're a monster! A monster. First Lily, now Helen."

"No, now you." He reached for her arm. "Enough of these games. It's time to end this once and for all."

Stacey kicked at him and he looked surprised as her foot came up and connected with his chest. The jolt surprised them both and the jarring in her leg sent a shaft of pain through her, but it shoved him back from her and his fingers slid away from her arm.

"What the hell do you think you're doing?" he asked, fighting to catch his breath.

"You won't toss me down any cliff again," she cried, balling up her fist and waving it at him. "I won't go easily."

He tried to reach for her and she kicked again, swinging her foot toward him and then the other, in rapid motions that he had trouble following. He might have size over her, but she had determination and as she connected with his leg, she realized the pain was diminishing now that she recognized what her movements needed to be. She aimed for the groin this time but he looked ready for that and stepped back. Her foot flicked at air and he lunged for it, missing her.

"Enough," he shouted and to her horror, he pulled a gun from his jacket pocket.

"You won't shoot me," she declared with more bravado than she felt. "A bullet hole will prove someone else did it."

"*If* they find your body," he said with a sneer. "But they won't. Not if it's weighted down with stones. Dear little Stacey will simply disappear." He gestured for her to walk toward the quarry. "Go.

That pool is bottomless beyond the rocks."

From behind him she saw movement through the branches and then a sandy head emerged from the forest. Fear choked her and she shook her head. "Mack..."

Carlos chortled. "He can't save you now. Not this time. And there's one last thing I want you to know. You were wrong. Mack is no longer totally consumed with Lily. You have managed to change that. But it's too late."

Was it? Mack held his finger to his lips and then to her horror, he moved forward. With a kick his foot hit the gun, knocking it out of Carlos' hand. The older man bellowed and whirled toward Mack. Stacey moved quickly, launching another kick at Carlos. When he jerked back in her direction, she kicked again, this time connecting with his groin, sending him to his knees.

Mack moved with more agility than she thought possible, lunging for the gun. Carlos scurried toward it too, but Stacey reached it first, kicking it toward Mack. With a shout, Carlos rose and charged toward her but she whirled and danced away. His shout behind her was horrifying and she spun around in time to see his momentum catapult him over the edge of the quarry. The sickening thud of his body hitting a rocky ledge and then another was something she knew she'd never forget. She hurried to the side in time to see his battered body bounce off another ledge before plummeting into the water below. It bobbed there, face down.

Her hands shook as she turned to Mack. "You...saved me."

His right hand clutched hers. "No. I think we saved each other."

They peered over the ledge at the lifeless body, and she sagged against Mack. He caught her with his right hand, wrapping his arm around her.

She leaned closer to him, pleased to be in his arms. Tears singed her eyes as she realized she never wanted to leave the protection of his touch again.

Mack kissed the top of her head. "We need to go back to the house and call the authorities. Are you strong enough to walk on your own?"

She nodded and together they began the trek back to the house. To her surprise and delight he kept his arm around her as though he didn't want to let her go either. Or maybe he didn't think she was capable of making it on her own. Only when they entered the house and he went to pick up the telephone did he relinquish his hold.

For Stacey the next two hours were agonizing. Mack insisted she stay at the house to answer questions for one sheriff's deputy while he took the others to the quarry. She outlined her story in shaky detail, her hands trembling and cold despite the hot cup of tea Mrs. D. gave her. As she spoke, she felt herself growing stronger. For once she felt like she had come through for Helen. She had uncovered the truth of her death and no one would ever again think that her friend committed suicide.

But she didn't feel total relief sweep through her until she saw Mack emerge from the woods. He walked with his limp more pronounced. She grabbed her jacket and ran out the door toward him.

He held out his hand, shaking his head. "It's over." His sigh was heavy, exhausted, but he had never looked better to her.

She flung herself to him and wrapped her arms around him. "I don't ever want to ever hear you say you can't do something," she said, leaning her head against his shoulder. Then realizing what she was doing, she straightened up. "I'm sorry."

His smile was tired, but there was light in his eyes. He stroked her face gently. "Don't be. You did it. You fixed me. And Carlos was right. When I left the house to look for you it was with the knowledge I'm no longer consumed with Lily. I said I wanted to wait for us to talk until we were finished, but now I'm not certain I even want to finish our project."

She looked up at him in surprise. "But you said it's what kept you going."

His eyes were warm as he looked down at her. "I found something else to do that." He squeezed her. "I think we need to have that talk later today. And tonight..."

She quivered with the thought of what he meant the night would hold. "Yes!" she said, the word bursting from her in a happy sputter.

He kissed the top of her forehead. "I want you so badly. From the first moment I saw you."

The comment was a little disheartening. What man might not want a naked woman. "When I was naked?"

He laughed and jostled her playfully. "You were naked? No. Don't even suggest that it was a physical reaction. Yes, you were quite lovely, a young vision. But what I remember was what I saw in your eyes. Those eyes as bottomless as that quarry back there. Sucked me in and trapped me. Forever."

Stacey felt like her insides would implode with happiness. "Forever?" she said breathlessly, realizing that she couldn't think of anything else to say for once. "Really? Forever?"

"If that's what you want. We can forget this project and you can help me with something else. Like my life. What do you say to a soak in that big tub of mine? I'd like to see you emerging from it and looking for a towel."

"Oh, yes." Tears spilled down her cheeks.

They turned together and walked toward Redfern Manor. The clouds were lifting and the gray stone house was framed in colorful new flower beds

Del was planting beside it. The grass was a brilliant green in the afternoon sun. As she grasped Mack's right hand and he squeezed hers back, she knew she had come home. The ghosts and the shadows dissipated as the thin veil of the mist lifted over the trees.

What would Kendra do now?

Stacey didn't care. She knew what she wanted to do. She turned and kissed Mack.

A word about the author...

Rebecca Grace is a former broadcast journalist who writes mystery and romantic suspense. Her 2010 book *Deadly Messages* from The Wild Rose Press was an Aspen Gold Finalist.

She also writes non-fiction and is a co-author of the handbook for authors, *10 Steps To Creating Memorable Characters*. She teaches writing classes and freelances in public relations. She currently lives in Littleton, Colorado.

Visit her online at www.rebeccagrace.com

Thank you for purchasing
this Wild Rose Press publication.
For other wonderful stories of romance,
please visit our on-line bookstore at
www.thewildrosepress.com.

For questions or more information
contact us at
info@thewildrosepress.com.

The Wild Rose Press
www.TheWildRosePress.com

To visit with authors of The Wild Rose Press
join our yahoo loop at
http://groups.yahoo.com/group/thewildrosepress/